ZOE EVANS

CHEER!

CONFESSIONS OF A WANNABE CHEERLEADER

ILLUSTRATED BY BRIGETTE BARRAGER

the coolest!

rahrah!

WITHDRAWN

LET'S GO! GRIZZLIES

Simon Spotlight
New York London Toronto Sydney

This book is a work of fiction. Any references to historical events, real people, or real locales are used fictitiously. Other names, characters, places, and incidents are the product of the author's imagination, and any resemblance to actual events or locales or persons, living or dead, is entirely coincidental.

 SIMON SPOTLIGHT

An imprint of Simon & Schuster Children's Publishing Division ★ 1230 Avenue of the Americas, New York, New York 10020 ★ Copyright © 2011 Simon & Schuster, Inc.

All rights reserved, including the right of reproduction in whole or in part in any form. SIMON SPOTLIGHT and colophon are registered trademarks of Simon & Schuster, Inc.

Text by Alexis Barad-Cutler

Designed by Giuseppe Castellano

For information about special discounts for bulk purchases, please contact Simon & Schuster Special Sales at 1-866-506-1949 or business@simonandschuster.com.

Manufactured in the United States of America 0611 OFF

First Edition 10 9 8 7 6 5 4 3 2 1

ISBN 978-1-4424-2241-4 (pbk)

ISBN 978-1-4424-2242-1 (eBook)

Library of Congress Catalog Card Number 2011924448

"Maaads." Mom cooed into my ear, shaking a pom-pom under my nose at the same time. This is how she's been waking me up every day since I was, like, three. And it's the same pom-pom. Between you and me, it's lost a few strings since its heyday and is starting to look really sad. "Big day today," she trilled. "Up! Up! Up!"

I opened my eyes and threw off the covers in **ÜBERFREAKOUT** mode. "What time is it? Am I late?" I scrambled toward my dresser to grab my contacts case. Not much gets me up on a Saturday with this much enthusiasm. Not much, that is, except the idea of tryouts for the Port Angeles school Titan cheerleaders. (OK, that and maybe the Farmers' Breakfast Special at the Pancake

farmer's breakfast

DEE-LISH!

GIVE ME A !!

House around the corner.) Trust me, it is **THAT GOOD.**

But back to why I was so excited about cheer tryouts. To start, a list of my favorite fun facts about cheerleading:

1) 3% of all female school athletes across the country are cheerleaders. Who knew?

2) 65% of all dangerous injuries in girls' school sports come from cheerleading. Insane!

3) 62% of cheerleaders are involved in a second sport. Overachievers much?

4) The first cheerleaders were men! Can you believe??

Mom was halfway inside my closet, selecting one of my red and white pairs of boy shorts and a tank (our school colors are red, white, and blue—patriotic much?) for me to wear to the tryouts. This is another one of our traditions—anything regarding cheerleading, Mom's allowed to help pick out my clothes. Every other occasion is off limits ever since I learned to use a sewing machine and discovered I have quite a killer fashion sense. And also,

GIVE ME A 2!

um, since I'm not five anymore.

"Madington, of course we're not late," she said, using a nickname I've warned her never to use when my friends are around. "We're an hour earlier than planned. Thought you'd want some time to digest the special whole-wheat pancakes I made you. I even put in some carob chips." She winked. "See you downstairs."

Mom laid my clothes on the bed and cheerily bounced out of my room, her wavy blond locks trailing behind her like a mermaid underwater. God, I L-O-V-E her hair.

Now might be a good time to mention that my mom is, like, absolutely gorgeous. I'm talking royalty pretty. No, seriously, she actually was homecoming queen AND prom queen in her day. Whenever she picks me up from school, I can always count on some guy or another to serenade us with that song "Stacy's Mom" that was popular a while back. They just substitute my name instead: "Maddy's mom has got it goin' on," and I just want to disappear in the front seat.

Oh, yeah. And she was a Titan. And she was captain

homecoming AND Prom

QUEEN

GIVE ME A 3!

of the cheerleading squad.

You could almost say my mom
and I have been preparing me for
today's tryouts ever since I was old
enough to wear her cheer uniform.
Well, I didn't exactly fit into it. I
was only three, and it dragged on
the floor behind me, but I was technically wearing it.
Every summer, while my friends were either lazing away
at camp or catching up on the latest comic books, I
was at cheer clinics, taking dance classes or tumbling
and stunting lessons, dreaming of the day I'd make it
onto the squad just like my mom. Which is why today's
tryouts were, like, everything I've been living for my
WHOLE LIFE! I'm pretty good at this cheer stuff
too. That is, when I'm not being spazzmadstic, which is
what my mom and I call it when I get all awkward and
mess up my moves.

Ok, so I guess I didn't get my mom's perfect cheer
genes.

I also didn't get her model looks. I mean, I'm not
saying that small children should be shielded from
looking at me! I'm not hideous or anything, but no guy
has ever told me I'm pretty, except for my friend
Evan—but we were five at the time and he was picking

GIVE ME A
4!

his nose while he said it, so I'm not entirely sure that counts. Five foot three is a totally average height for a girl my age, and my eyes are this really cool light green, which is pretty rare. My wavy brown hair? That I wouldn't mind changing up. Eduardo, the guy who cuts Mom's and my hair, says my hair is "honey colored," like that's supposed to make me like it more, but I don't see much of a difference between the color of my hair and the color of the wood floor in our den, and I still totally wish Mom would let me dye it something dramatic like red or black. But she won't. I do like my freckles, though—and they really come out right before cheer season, because that's when I'm practicing outside the most (obvs).

In the car on the way to school, I selected some pump-it-up music on my iPod to get me psyched and to calm my nerves a little.

"Mads, turn it down. Even _I_ can hear it," Mom said in that disapproving parental tone.

I pretended to turn the music down by rubbing my hands in the general direction of my iPod. This is a great thing about the older generation, as I like to refer to them. They don't know the first thing about how to operate anything with "pod" or "pad" or "i" in its name. Mom still has this giant tower of CDs in our living

room, plus big fat books of CD collections. I keep telling
her that CDs are so 1997, but she won't listen to me.
Anyway, I don't ever have to worry about Mom snooping
in my iPhone or (one day, hopefully, when I get one) my
iPad. Not like she would, though. She's chill about those
kinds of things.

Anyway, I started to think
about what it would be like to
make it onto the team. How
amazing it would be to walk
down the halls of PAS as a
bona fide Titan, with peeps
like Katie Parker, Hilary Cho,
and Clementine Prescott
having my back. I mean, they're
not the nicest people in the world, but I don't think
they're as bad as everyone thinks they are. People don't
understand the kind of pressure they're under—giving
every ounce of their physical strength to cheer on the
Titans, not to mention all those supergrueling cheer
competitions. It's enough to make someone lose it.

I mean, it's not like I want to be all besties with
them. But to learn from the best cheerleaders?
To earn respect from the best? To BE the best?
THAT I can totally see. And I would so love to wear

GIVE ME A
6!

that white, red, and blue skirt. It's adorbs.

"Madington, we're here."

It was weird. . . . Mom's voice sounded like it was coming from so far away. I hate being woken from perfect daydreams. Especially when the reality was that cheer tryouts were just minutes away. Hello, butterflies?

"You're going to be fabulous," she said, giving my arm a squeeze.

The gym smelled—as usual—like the bottom of an old Crayola box mixed with armpit sweat. Delish! I tried to tell myself that I was ready. I had my journal in my silver and gold gym bag for inspiration (with all my notes on cheers, stunt sequences, routines, and general thoughts on life—oh, and my fashion designs ☺), and not a single lump stood out in my ponytail. Whatever Katie and Clementine threw my way, I could handle. Right?

Hmm, well, maybe not.

As soon as I saw the other girls, aka the competition, stretching out on the mats, I got a little nervous. There was Katarina Tarasov, the Russian exchange student I'd heard about. She just started school with us this year. I heard she was practically Olympics material back wherever she was from.

I watched her practicing perfectly arched backflips across the mat.

"Hey, nice job," I told her as I walked by.

"You're welcome!" she said, smiling proudly.

Unfortunately she doesn't speak much English. I decided to avoid sharing mat space with her that morning. I didn't feel like teaching an Introduction to English class in addition to trying out.

"All right, girls," said Coach Whipley. (Isn't it funny how coaches always tend to have the most appropriate names?) "It's gonna go like this. Katie and Hilary are going to lead you through a dance routine. Then Clementine will teach you a cheer. Then you'll perform each as a group. The last part of tryouts will be individual tumbling and gymnastics. Clear?"

It was exactly what I had planned for. No curveballs. Phew.

The routine was set to a medley of songs by Rihanna, Pink, and Lady Gaga. Unfortunately, I had stuck myself next to Jared "It's Showtime!" Handler, whose interpretation of every move was sprinkled with outrageous jazz hands and Fred Astaire footwork. I couldn't believe he actually showed up for tryouts. I'd heard him telling everyone he was going to go for cheer this year when he didn't get any lead roles in

GIVE ME AN 8!

last spring's <u>West Side Story</u>. I'd secretly been hoping he was joking. Not that I mind people going for new things, but I don't like that he's just using cheer to give him an edge for drama class.

All through the dance routine, led by the amazing Hilary, Jared kept bumping into me and ruining my already-compromised-on-a-regular-day rhythm. I was so worried he was going to accidentally slap me with those jazz hands that I kept flinching. I missed a couple of steps in the middle of the routine and messed up a turn that normally would have been fine for me if I'd been able to concentrate fully. I looked like I was being electrocuted!! I swear, at next year's <u>Once Upon a Mattress</u> production I'm going to sit in the front row on opening night and rap Eminem while Jared sings lead.

I totally aced the cheer, but during the individual tumbling and jumping in front of the judges, I became Awkward Girl and seriously spazzmadsed out. I accidentally hit my toe to my nose during a toe jump and even saw Clementine snicker. My triple backflip became a back **FLOP** in the last second because my hand caught on a weird piece of the mat (just my luck). By that time I had, like, zero confidence, so when the judges asked me to do a front handspring I didn't get enough height off the ground and **FREAKED**

GIVE ME A 9!

in midair, folding into a tumble instead. At this point, everyone was watching me in stunned silence. Like, the **WHOLE GYM**. I don't think anyone has ever had a worse cheer tryout. Even poor old Tabitha Sue Stevens—who can't even do a split (a regular one, like, on the floor)—looked sorry for me.

"That was . . . interesting. Thank you, Madison Hays," said Coach Whipley. And her face was all "what a loser," I could tell. I seriously wanted to burrow into the mat and just die. All that work, all those summers, for nada. My mom would be sooooo disappointed.

We weren't allowed to leave the gym until all the tryouts were over, so I suffered through the rest of the morning watching everyone else do way better than me and pictured my soon-to-be cheerless existence. I'd spend the rest of my life being a cheer wannabe. I'd probably end up a crazy old lady, still wearing her cheer uniform and grumbling, "I could have been something!" And when I died, people would feel sorry for me and bury me with my pom-poms.

"No!" I shouted.

"Huh?" grunted Jacqueline Sawyer, one of the Titan cheerleaders, who happened to be sitting near me.

"Oh, nothing." I blushed. I hadn't realized that I'd said that out loud. Sometimes I do that, though.

My daydreams can get pretty intense.

Jacqueline just looked at me like I had three heads. I figured I might as well get used to it, since that's how everyone will start looking at me after hearing I had the

WORST CHEERLEADING TRYOUT EVER.

"It's not <u>that</u> bad, you know," Jacqueline said, leaning in.

"What do you mean?" I asked. Was this chick reading my mind? Spoooooky.

"You'll still be cheering, just for a slightly different squad," Jacqueline said mysteriously.

Then it was my turn to look at her like she was from another planet. And then the realization hit me.

OH. NO.

The Grizzlies!!!

Jacqueline smirked and turned her attention back to the tryouts when she saw that I understood.

So, all the kids who don't make the Titans are automatically placed onto the Grizzlies, aka the B-squad, aka the rejects. I had completely forgotten about the school policy against turning anyone away from wanting to participate in school-spirit activities. The Grizzlies cheered for the school teams the Titans were too proud to cheer for: swim team, debate team, chess club, etc. In other words: Loserville! Last year, as a prank, some guys threw dog biscuits at the Grizzlies during a swim meet. Like I said, it's a world of NO. Love of cheerleading or not, I was NOT going to be a big, fat, hairy Grizzly.

I prayed that by some miracle my name would be on that magical sheet of paper outside Coach Whipley's office at the end of the day, securing my fate as a glorious and magnificent Titan.

Guess what? It wasn't. I must have stared at the paper, for like, ten minutes straight. I even tried walking away and quickly whipping around, hoping that my sneak attack would somehow shift the ink in my favor. It didn't work. My name was so NOT on there. Want to know where my name was? That's right. On the big, fat, hairy Grizzlies list! Sandwiched between Jared Handler and Tabitha Sue Stevens. Go figure.

Now all the new cheerleaders are running to their parents' cars, squealing with excitement. My heart can't sink any lower into my chest.

"I see you at the practice Monday, yes?"

I turned around and saw Katarina, her gym bag

GIVE ME A 12!

draped over her thin shoulders. I just shrugged in reply. I wonder if she understood. Either way, if I **AM** going to see her at practice on Monday, I figure I can wait till then to start our English lessons.

Here comes my mom's car. Her expectant, smiling face is breaking my heart! What will she say when she finds out? She'll probably be mortified. This much I know is true: Pigs will fly before I become a Grizzly Bear.

I am meant to be a Titan.

Spirit Level:

Run Over by the Football Team

I didn't mean to slam the door that hard when I got into Mom's prized silver Jetta, but I was so angry at myself for not making the team, I guess my anger gave me some kind of Hulk-like strength. Me Angry Madison. Me Break Your Car!!!

"Oh, Mads," Mom said when she saw my face. "I'm sorry."

"Yeah. Sucks."

"Want to talk about it?" she asked.

"No. Later. Maybe."

My being angry meant that I was only speaking in one-word sentences. I also really wasn't in the mood to be around Mom just then. I didn't need a reminder of what a superawesome cheerleader looks like, compared with what a totally spastic, can't-keep-it-together-for-one-tryout cheerleader looks like. I figured

GIVE ME A 14!

staring out the window at the suburban scenery of our neighborhood—minimall, post office, elementary school— might take my mind off the morning's disappointment.

Mom reached out and tickled the back of my neck like she always does when I'm upset. I shrugged her away.

"Hon, I'm sure you were amazing out there," she said, her voice more upbeat than I knew she was feeling. We both had worked too hard for today to be let down like this. "We'll keep training just like we always do, and you'll just try out in the spring. You have plenty of Titan years ahead of you still. What's so bad about that?"

I looked over at her and raised my eyebrow skeptically. See, Mom knows how important it is to me to be a Titan, just like she had been. After the hundreds of stories she's told me my whole life about being a Titan cheerleader, she totally knew how "bad" it was.

"Mom, it's just not that simple. Right now, I'm on the Grizzlies. As in Grizzly Bears. Do you even know what that means?"

Her silence was enough of an answer.

"It's the reject team, Mom. It's where all the kids who don't make the Titans go to cheer for the school's other rejects. Mom, if you saw the other kids on that

GIVE ME A 15!

list, you'd <u>die</u>. One girl can't even speak English, let alone cheer!"

Mom let out a deep sigh. Thankfully, I'd reached her inner Titan.

"Wow. I see. Ok. Well, I still think you're going to want to try out again next year. You'll have an extra year of experience under your belt. We'll sign you up for more cheer camps, maybe some private classes—"

I couldn't take it anymore. I was cheered out—at least for the day.

"Mom! Stop. Just . . . I don't feel like talking about it right now, ok?"

She nodded, finally getting it. I turned the volume up on my iPod, but unfortunately, my pump-it-up mix was still playing from earlier that morning. Yeah, this was really not a pump-it-up kinda moment for me. It's funny how things can change so quickly. One minute, you'll be listening to a song and thinking about how awesome the rest of the day could turn out. And then, the next time you listen to that same song, something unbelievably awful could have happened. Like someone might have stuck their jazz hands in your face so that you totally spazzed out during your cheer routine and then you didn't make the squad!!! **WHAT IS WRONG WITH ME!?!**

GIVE ME A 16!

Then it hit me: I've been so naive. The Titans were surely on the lookout for cheerleaders they can take to the Nationals competition this year. If that's the kind of cheerleader the Titans want, it's no wonder they picked right over me. (Well, that and the fact that I totally blew my tryout.) Like I said, I'm a good cheerleader—better than good. But to be a Titan? You have to be uh-mazing. A Nationals-worthy cheerleader doesn't mess up **EVER**. She hits her stunts on cue perfectly and has flawless dismounts. She's the kind of cheerleader Katie Parker, Clementine Prescott, and Hilary Cho are. The kind of cheerleader Mom was.

And what kind of cheerleader am I? I'm Spazzmadstic Madison. Jazzhands Jared or no Jared, I would have messed up just fine on my own.

By the time we pulled up onto our cobblestone driveway, I felt like ten tons of bricks had just fallen on top of my head.

"I'm gonna lie down upstairs."

Mom just nodded and let me be.

Along the stairwell, Mom keeps pictures of me through the years in all

GIVE ME A 17!

my dance and cheerleading outfits. My best friend, Lanie Marks, calls it "Maddy Alley" because it's just pictures of little ol' me straight through from the first stair to the last.

Embarrassingly enough, Lanie has actually known me since the first picture, at the bottom of the stairs, was taken. I actually remember us at age four, both wearing our tuxedo outfits for our tap dance recital. It was one of those numbers where everyone got a top hat and cane for a very dumbed-down, toddlerized "Singin' in the Rain" routine. Unfortunately almost everyone in our class was rather uncoordinated, being four and all. One girl poked the boy next to her with her cane repeatedly until he cried. A couple kids' hats fell off their heads in the middle of the dance, and this one boy kept on picking them up and returning them to each kid like it was his job. Lanie and I were the only ones who stuck with the routine the entire time as the rest of our class fell apart around us. I guess that was the moment that brought us together: the whole world falling apart around us, and the two of us sticking together. Kind of funny, huh?

That was also the first and last time Lanie had ever taken a dance class. She firmly believes that, ahem, and I quote, "the only kind of energy that one

GIVE ME AN 18!

should expend is intellectual energy." I also remember
Lanie being excited about not having to wear a girlie
costume to that recital—and to this day I can't
remember having seen her in anything other than pants
or knee-grazing shorts. On the outside, Lanie and I are
really different.

Today, the pictures in Maddy Alley, which always
used to give me a sense of pride as I walked past
them, only made me furious. There's me, age six, hands
on my hips in a flapper dress right before I performed
at my jazz recital. And there's another picture of
me at nine, when Mom let me dye a streak of my hair
pink to match my pink leotard for my gymnastics
competition. I tried to spring up the stairs past the
pictures as quickly as possible. Nine-year-old me didn't
know that all those competitions would be for nothing.

GIVE ME A
19!

Around 8 p.m. I woke up to the feeling of weight shifting on my bed. I didn't even realize I'd fallen asleep! Mom was sitting next to me, looking at me with a funny expression. She looked a little worried and a little sad.

"You ok?" she asked.

"Not really," I said.

"Want to watch Bring It On?"

(Sidebar: Bring It On is my all-time fave movie in the entire world. So, she really was bringing out the big guns. Me refusing a Bring It On opportunity is like the Titans refusing new uniforms, which they would obvs **NEVER** do.)

Mom picked up my journal from next to my pillow. I'd been leafing through it before passing out, trying to figure out what went wrong. She smoothed the back of the journal with her hand.

"So, you've made your decision, huh, Madington? No Grizzlies for you?"

"Are you kidding? I'm not even considering it." I turned my pillow to the cool side and lay down on it exasperatedly. "Mom. Seriously."

Then she started to get that lilt in her voice that tells me she's going to try to convince me to do something I don't want to do but she thinks will be good for me.

GIVE ME A 20!

"Well, it would be a shame if all these amazing cheers just sat here getting dusty."

I turned to look at her.

"Just think, Mads. If these kids are as bad as you say they are, don't you think they could use a <u>real</u> cheerleader on their team? Think about how awful they'll look out there on their own without any guidance. Can these cheerleaders even do simple things? Like jumps? Or a pyramid? Who's going to teach them not to 'suck' so badly?"

I thought about the squad and its current roster of cheerleaders. From what I saw at tryouts today, the situation is grim. Jared is as scrawny as a kindergartner. He can't lift an iPod, let alone a one-hundred-pound flyer. That is, if there are any flyers on this sorry squad. And Tabitha Sue (better known as Toxic Tabitha to most of the school ever since an unfortunate bathroom-related accident in elementary school), well, she'd started sweating and puffing by the fifteen-second mark of the dance routine. Katarina did an awesome job on all the tumbling and stunt parts of tryouts, but she couldn't follow the cheer at all. When we were all cheering together, Coach Whipley scrunched her nose as if she smelled something foul, and asked, "Is someone speaking Russian?" I have to

GIVE ME A
2!!

give it to Katarina for cheering despite the odds.
Now that's dedication. But still. That wasn't reason
enough for me to get involved in a motley crew of bad
cheerleaders.

I sat up in bed. "Ok, so I'd be teaching them how to
cheer, like, out of the goodness of my heart? I don't
get it. What does this do for me?" I crossed my arms
over my chest.

Seriously, what was Mom expecting me to
be, the Mother Teresa of cheerleaders?

Mom looked at me, her eyes wide with
optimism. "Just think how much you would
stand out from the crowd. You would be the
best cheerleader on that team, no doubt.
And at every game, you'd be the one
everyone would notice. Don't you think
the Titans would eventually notice?"

And that's when Mom's plan actually started sounding halfway decent. I'll easily be the best Grizzly on that team, and during practices the Titans will be able to see what I'm really made of. I might not be ready for Nationals, but I'm definitely ready to be a Titan. And maybe if I just work a little harder, split a little wider, cheer a little louder, I can even get noticed and recruited by the Titans—possibly even by spring!

I picked up my journal and started sketching out a plan for the first week of practice. I looked up and saw Mom smiling at me. She bounced up from the bed and announced that she was going to make some popcorn with hot chilies in it.

"Your favorite," she said, winking before she walked out of my room.

I guess on Monday I'll be a proud member of the Grizzly Bears. Just don't expect me to stop shaving my legs or anything.

GIVE ME A 23!

Barf!

Lanie met me in the "Lounge" after second-period classes. The "Lounge" is a designated hangout spot for our grade. The grades above us have their own designated areas, too, but this is the first year we've ever had a space of our own. If you value your life, you will never be caught sitting in, stepping foot in, even breathing on, any grade's turf before you're officially allowed.

(BTW, the "Lounge" consists of a corner near the cafeteria entrance, where two blocks of concrete covered in some kind of felt form benches. It's not like there are any fancy throw pillows or mood lighting. But it might as well be a VIP club, for the amount of anticipation everyone feels waiting for that one day that he or she is finally able to call it their own.)

GIVE ME A 24!

We arranged ourselves on the highest of the
benches to get the best view of everyone walking by.

"Have you seen Alison Bunker yet?" asked Lanie,
leaning back on her palms.

"No, should I have?"

"Looks like she's decided to leave the prepsters
behind and join the goths. I can't stand when people
think they can change teams just because they've
changed clothes, like all it is is a fashion statement.
Like, 'Oooh, now I wear black nail polish! I'm so hardcore.
This is the real me!'" Lanie rolled her eyes. As much as
she pretended not to care at all, Lanie seemed to be in
the know about all the different social groups within
our school—who was emo, skater, punk, goth, preppy,
jock, you name it. She was an expert, also, on what
group each person had previously inhabited. One of her
biggest pet peeves is the poseur. Another pet peeve is

GIVE ME A
25!

people who try to label Lanie Marks.

"Hey, whatever floats her boat," I said. "Maybe she's always been a goth kid trapped inside a prepster's body." I know how to egg Lanie on. She was about to get started on another rant when she realized I was just trying to annoy her on purpose. Hee, hee.

"Oh, don't even start with me Cheer-Pants," Lanie said, slapping my leg. "So," she continued, focusing her eyes on my journal. "You still going all Grizzly on us?"

I'd told her last night on video chat about my big plan for the year. How I am going to stick with being a Grizzly Bear so I can be the best cheerleader on the team and get noticed by the Titans. She's not a huge fan of girls like Clementine, Katie, or Hilary—the Royal Triumvirate, as she calls them. But she totally supported my decision when I told her about it, like she always does when it comes to cheer stuff.

"Yep, still going Grizzly. Rawr." I made a claw at her face.

"Sweet," said Lanie. "I've got to say, you're a trooper. From what you told me last night, the team sounds kind of rough."

"I know," I agreed. To me, it's a small price to pay, ultimately, in order to realize my biggest goal in life. "Think you could stop by today during

GIVE ME A 26!

practice for moral support?"

"Oh, I am so going to be there!" exclaimed Lanie. "I need to report back to Evan and let him know if this situation is as grizzly as we think it is. Wink wink . . . get it?"

Evan Andrews is our best guy friend. He joined our little crew in kindergarten, when Lanie and I were playing house at recess and needed a husband to complete our family. Since this was much more enticing than being "it" during games of tag, he immediately agreed to play the part, and we've been inseparable ever since. These days, when he's not buying a comic book, talking about a comic book, or researching one online, he's usually reading one. Every year, Evan spends the money he earns at his summer job (wait for it . . . working at a comic book store! Big surprise ☺) on going to this giant comic-book convention in San Diego. It's like Disneyland for dorks—the kind who make up their own alien languages and who have crushes on blue women with three eyes.

"Ha-ha. He's been sending me these dumb texts all morning with stupid jokes about it being hunting season, and saying stuff like, 'Watch out for bears!'" I told Lanie.

"Yeah, when I told him you were joining the Grizzly

GIVE ME A
27!

squad, he laughed so hard that he nearly squirted milk out of his nose."

I don't know why this annoyed me, but it did. I guess maybe I'm a little hurt that he was making fun of my decision. I thought Evan, of all people, would understand what it means to commit to something utterly and entirely, even if people think it's kind of nerdy. I mean, seriously. Comic-book conventions? Who is he to laugh at me?!

Here's another important thing to know about Evan: Even though he dresses like a slightly messy male librarian, I think that if he tried just a little harder, he really could have potential. There have been times, and I can't say exactly why, when I've felt a tiny bit more than "just friends" about him. Like, I'll look at him and be like, "Hmm. Kinda cute!" and then the moment passes, and I'm like, "Whoa! Where did that come from?" and he's back to being just Evan, my guy friend, again. It's really weird.

Librarian

Cute!

GIVE ME A 28!

"Well, he'll have to slurp that milk back up when he sees me standing on the top of a Titan pyramid this time next year. Or maybe sooner. Who knows?" I said smugly.

Just then, Lanie caught a scrawny seventh grader walking too close to the perimeter of our "Lounge." (In his defense, I think he was just trying to throw a soda can away.)

"Excuse me," she said, clearing her throat loudly. The scrawny kid looked up at her with his soda can frozen above the trash can. "Your foot?" she said, pointing to how close his toe had gotten to a punishable offense.

"I—I—I'm sorry," he stuttered before scuttling away, still holding the can.

"Lanes!" I exclaimed. "That was just mean. You're just as bad as the people we used to hate."

"The people we used to hate did **EXACTLY** that to us when we were his age," she said, folding her arms across her chest.

"That so doesn't make it right," I said, smiling at my friend.

Lanie exhaled. "No, but it does make it fair. And did you see the look on his face? Priceless, huh?"

I laughed. "Can't deny it. That was pretty funny."

GIVE ME A 29!

Spirit Level!

Nursing Bruises

OMG, OMG, OMG. THIS WAS THE WORST IDEA EVER! This squad is pathetic! They're not even good enough to cheer on the debate team. Seriously, we're so sad, we make the math league look cool.

At first I was somewhat hopeful. I was jogging up toward where the Grizzlies were assembled on the sports field and saw, off in the distance, a large figure lifting another solidly built person up in the air. "Oh, cool," I thought. "Two new guys joined the Grizzlies, and they're actually strong. Maybe they'll make good bases." But as I got closer I realized that these weren't just any two guys. These were Ian McClusky and Matt Herrington, aka the Testosterone Twins. They're two of the biggest football jocks in the school, and last year they thought it would be har dee har har funny if they duct taped a couple of dorky Grizzly guys to

GIVE ME A 30!

the benches inside the locker room after practice one day. Apparently, as punishment, their coach banned them from football this year and sentenced them to join the Grizzlies to see what it felt like. Of course, until that moment I had been too busy thinking about my quick ascent to Titanhood to remember certain important details—like who I'll have to whip into shape in order to make it there.

"You're so dead!" Ian said as he punched Matt's chest with a thud.

"Hey!" I snapped, coming into the circle of my new teammates. Ian wiped the back of his hand across his wide forehead, his eyes narrowing in on me. "Last I checked, you were on a cheerleading squad, not a football team," I said to him.

"Yeah, whatever," Ian replied, giving Matt a halfhearted noogie.

UGH. Eye roll.

Ms. Burger (or Ms. Booger, as everyone prefers to call her), the faculty adviser for our team, was desperately trying to organize the team into a warm-up. Ordinarily she is a Life Studies teacher—the kind that's notorious for making each girls' class watch the same cringeworthy Your Changing Body DVD each year. Ms. Burger is the kind of person who collects desk calendars with pictures of

GIVE ME A
3!!

bridges on them: bridges over waterfalls, bridges along a small country road, city bridges. I don't really know exactly what kind of person that makes her, because I've never met anyone else who collects bridge desk calendars. All I know is that when she takes a liking to something, she gets totally fixated. Last year, Lanie and I bought her a calendar with horses on it, just to see if she'd switch it up. She didn't.

My point: Whoever decided Ms. Burger was the right person to coach a misfit group of coed cheerleaders must have been kidding.

"All right everyone, this pamphlet says here that we should start with a series of basic stretches," Ms. Burger said, lowering her glasses down on the bridge of her nose and holding the yellowed and dog-eared pamphlet an arm's length away from her body. I glanced at the cover of it. It actually said, "How to Run a Cheerleading Practice" and was dated 1958—which might as well have been the Stone Age of Cheer, if you ask me.

"Hey, Ms. Burger, I'll just lead the team, if you don't mind," I said. I think I heard a collective sigh of relief. I don't think anyone wanted to see our Life Studies teacher doing a front split in the short shorts she decided to sport that afternoon.

GIVE ME A 32!

Ms. Burger gratefully took a seat on the bleachers and read a book for the rest of practice. Guess what was on the cover. That's right, a picture of a bridge!

During knee touches, Matt shouted, "Gross, man!" and began waving his hand around his face like tiny killer wasps were attacking him.

"Naw, dude. Wasn't me!" said Ian.

I glared at both of them.

"Sick," mumbled Matt.

Everyone immediately had this look of "Hey, it wasn't me," including Katarina. (Note to self: I guess there is a universal gesture for "Hey, something smells gross.") Tabitha Sue was the only one left looking a little guilty. Her face started to get really red, and the top of her forehead was beaded with sweat. Poor Tabitha Sue.

"All right, guys. Lunges," I told the group, hoping to distract the team with a more painful stretch. I could see the Titans across the field, doing their own stretches in their perfect-looking uniforms, with their crisply pleated skirts and flattering tank tops.

arm-flattering tank top

Sparkly and NEW!

stretchy fabric

bouncy pleated skirt

GIVE ME A 33!

The colors on their uniforms never seem to fade since, of course, they get new ones every year. Which also means that their uniform keeps up with the latest in cheer fashion. Translation: Their skirts get shorter every year. The Grizzlies have been inheriting the same ones for who knows how many years. If I had to rate ours on the looks scale, they would fall somewhere between "butt" and "ugly." Oh, and let's discuss the smell for a second. Picture this: Grizzlies in the past must have let a bunch of smelly truck drivers use their uniforms to dry their sweaty armpits, then they must have cleaned a couple

hole!

arm hole too sma

too short

wrinkled!

ITCHY, SMELLY, STAINED!

makes your butt look HUG

too long

of toilets with them. Then I'm imagining they hung them to dry in a barn. And that's my not-so-horrifying version of the story. I had to douse mine in Victoria's Secret Live Pink body spray, even though I've already washed it ten times in a row.

One of the better cheerleading Titan guys was already leading the team through their jumps at the other end of the field as Katie went up to each

GIVE ME A 34!

cheerleader to correct his or her posture. Their practices were notoriously grueling and serious, and the rumor is, they get harder every year. The weary looks on the cheerleaders' faces at the end of practice usually says it all. Just when they think they're completely spent—after tumbling, jumps, choreography, and stunts—Katie will make the Titans review their latest cheers and write new ones. I looked back at my own team. Tabitha Sue was almost out of breath, and we hadn't even started tumbling yet.

"Madison?" Jared called out after we had gotten through a few rounds of pretty pathetic jumps. "Are we going to start some choreography today? I was thinking maybe something by the Artist Formerly Known as Prince. I even worked something up last night," he said excitedly. Jared then launched into a shimmy, touched the floor, and threw his head back dramatically. "What do you think?"

We all looked at him in stunned silence.

"Ahem. Lo-hoser!" Matt coughed under his breath.

"It's . . . um . . . cool," I said, trying not to be outwardly judgmental. "I don't know if it's exactly cheer material, though. Maybe we could consider it for something later?"

Jared pouted.

GIVE ME A 35!

"Do you guys maybe want to try a pyramid?" I asked hopefully.

Most of the team stared back at me with quizzical looks.

I decided to demonstrate with myself, Ian, and Matt because I figured they were the strongest guys on the team for now. We were standing toward the edge of the track area, and occasionally runners were jogging by throughout practice, but I wasn't paying much attention.

I showed Ian and Matt what they were going to do. As I climbed into the pyramid, I could tell I was a little unbalanced. But I wanted so badly to show the team that I knew what I was doing, I refused to admit defeat. Although, to be honest, I don't think the Testosterone Twins paid all that much attention during my pyramid tutorial. Everything kind of happened in slow motion. I could feel myself sort of falling backward, and instead of my teammates spotting me and catching me at my waist, I fell for what seemed like minutes, watching the puffy white clouds above me until my vision was obscured by a figure whizzing by in red sweatpants.

Bam! Face-to-knee collision.

"Urrrggggg." I mumbled incoherently.

GIVE ME A 36!

My body lay half on the track and half on the grass.

Then a gorgeous vision peered over me. He had brown wavy hair and eyes the color of my favorite gelato flavor—espresso chocolate, the kind with 70% dark chocolate in it. The late-afternoon sun was hitting the back of his head so that he had this bright orange halo of light all around his face, and for a minute I thought maybe I'd died and this was the angel welcoming me into heaven's gates. "Hmm, ok. I'll take it," I thought.

"You ok?" the angel asked, leaning over me. He moved a little to the right, and the halo disappeared. Phew. Ok, not dead. And that's when I felt the throbbing in my nose. "Ow" was my only response.

He brought one of his perfectly chiseled arms behind his head to scratch his neck, accentuating a biceps. I secretly hoped he did that on purpose to impress me. It's true, half of what boys do is kind of just their autopilot. But once in a while, between the burping and farting, they manage to work something really cute into their repertoire of actions too.

Ms. Burger started searching for injuries, asking me questions about internal bleeding. But I hardly noticed, because I was too busy admiring the curve of the angel's nose.

GIVE ME A
37!

"Bevan Ramsey," Ms. Burger scolded, "I'm surprised at you. How did you just run into an entire cheerleading pyramid?"

"Bevan," I thought to myself. Right—that IS his name. He's been in my grade for years, but I don't ever remember him looking quite like this. I don't remember ever seeing those biceps before. . . .

"Hey, I'm really sorry," he said, looking at me.

"I was in the zone, Ms. Burger," he said. "And to be honest, I wasn't really sure what it was they were doing," he said, a little apologetically.

I started to sit up, putting my hand to my nose. Katarina came by my side and held out a pocket mirror so I could assess the damage. (It's NOT pretty.)

"Is it broken?" I asked no one in particular, hoping maybe someone had medical training.

"Nope, I don't think so," said Bevan, looking closely at my face. "I've had, like, five broken noses from sports injuries. That doesn't look broken to me," he answered, showing a nearly perfect smile with one really adorable gap in his bottom teeth.

"Hey, dude!" someone shouted from the other end of the track. "You comin'?"

Bevan brushed off his sweatpants and stretched one of his perfect biceps across his chest.

GIVE ME A
38!

"Again, sorry, um. . . . What's your name?"

"Madison," I said, the embarrassment of the situation hitting me all of a sudden. I actually fell onto that gorgeous creature. OMG!

He started to jog away but turned and said, "Ice always helps, by the way," then ran off down the track.

Thank goodness at that point Lanie appeared by the bleachers, because I just could not have handled the rest of practice without her making stupid faces at me. And she was wearing her "ironic" pigtails, which made for even more comic relief because she was able to pull them and blow her cheeks out at the same time, which is one of my fave Lanie moves.

We tried the pyramid a couple more times—far away from the edge of the track—and it took a lot to convince people to be flyers after seeing my heinous fall. The Twins either grabbed ankles too roughly or reached for inappropriate places on people's bodies. SO. GROSS. Jared wanted to try, because he liked the idea of

GIVE ME A
39!

hitting the pose at the top of the pyramid. He called it "the showstopper."

"Uh, yeah. No way are we touching him," said Matt, crossing his arms defiantly.

I tried to spot Jared along with Tabitha Sue, but Jared mistakenly picked Tabitha Sue's nose as he nearly lost his balance while he lifted his hand out and up.

At the end of practice, I wearily trudged toward Lanie.

"Jeez, Lanes, I knew practice was gonna be bad, but I didn't think it was gonna be that bad."

"Even worse than we suspected, huh?" said Lanie. "Ooh, Mads. What happened to your nose?"

"Yeah, embarrassing story, actually. I fell onto Bevan Ramsey," I said, shaking my head. "But not, like, in a romantic way. I kind of collided with him," I clarified. I waved good-bye to my teammates, who were making their way off the field.

I told Lanie what happened, and she couldn't help but laugh at me. I totally would too if I were her.

"I thought he played soccer," said Lanie.

That was my Lanes. On top of every social group, including the sports guys. But still, I was surprised. "Even I didn't know that, and I'm supposed to be a cheerleader."

GIVE ME A 40!

She shrugged. "Well, he's pretty popular. Word gets around, I guess. Where've you been hiding?"

"I can't tell you how helpful you're being in raising my morale right now. But seriously, I don't know how I didn't really notice him before," I said. "And now," I whispered, "I think I'm a teeny bit in love with him."

"Ok, whatever." Lanie laughed, checking her phone for messages. "Let's talk next week and see if this lasts longer than your last crush."

She did have a point. The last guy I liked was Sean Kwong, who was part of the skater posse. We shared a moment one day in study hall, and after that I downloaded pics of him from Facebook and inserted my face next to his on iPhoto. The next week, I actually saw him skate, and let's just say he is one of those guys who wears his skateboard as an accessory. I guess I kinda share Lanie's distaste for poseurs.

"Hey," said Lanie, "I don't have to be home till eight thirty. You want to go to the shack?" she asked. The shack is a place around the corner from school that has outdoor seating and order-at-the-counter service. On almost any night of the week you can find, like, half the school there.

"Nah," I said. "Maybe another night." I looked at where the Titans were still going strong. "I'm going to

GIVE ME A 4!!

stay and practice some stuff I didn't get to do today."

"No worries," said Lanie. "I'll hit up Evan."

I said good-bye and started on some backflips. I know it's kind of loser-y, but I pretended that I was a Titan and that Katie had just asked me to go farther down the field, where I'd have more space to flip.

"Yep," I said under my breath, looking at the corner that my very challenged team had occupied just a little while before. If anyone should still be practicing, it's the Grizzlies.

"Lots of space here. A whole team's worth."

GIVE ME A
42!

Tuesday, September 7

Dinnertime, my room

Spirit Level:

Feelin' F-O-U-L

Dad called tonight. Whoop dee doo . He wants to take me to dinner on Friday with Beth, his new "friend." Can't wait! Gag, gag. Mom says I should learn to have a better "team attitude" when it comes to our family. I tried to tell her that the team attitude is one thing when it comes to cheer, quite another when it comes to your dad's new girlfriend. She laughed when I said that, and I know she totally agrees with me but can't admit it because she's trying to take the high road.

"So? Did you make the team?" Dad asked me as I climbed on top of our granite kitchen counter next to the phone on the wall. Mom refuses to get a cordless. I think she likes to eavesdrop on my conversations with Dad.

I know he was just asking out of obligation. First of all, I'm positive Mom already briefed him on my joining the Grizzlies, because that's just something she would

GIVE ME A 43!

do. Second, he doesn't really approve of my obsession with cheerleading. He never liked it when Mom was into cheerleading either. Well, I think he did at first. See, they were high school sweethearts. He was the football jock, and she was the hot cheerleader. It's a cliché, but I guess there's a reason for clichés, right? I think the problem for him was that she was still fiercely loyal to cheerleading even after they left high school. According to Mom, he didn't understand why she sometimes traveled to cheerleading competitions long after her days of cheering were over. When I was little, I even remember them fighting over Mom wanting to sign me up for gymnastics class—which I was, like, begging them to do. Dad was all about signing me up for science camp, where activities included collecting bugs and making volcanoes out of vinegar. And I hated bugs. I still do.

"No, Dad, I didn't make the Titans." I sighed into the phone, wrapped the cord around my pinky, and began twirling. "But I decided to stick with it and joined this other team called the Grizzly Bears."

"Grizzly Bears?" Dad laughed. "What, do they put out forest fires and cheer at the same time?"

"Ha-ha," I said. "No, they're, like, this B-squad of cheerleaders. They basically suck, but I'm hoping to change that a little. And to stand out so that maybe the

GIVE ME A
44!

Titans will pick me to be on the team later in the year."

Dad was quiet on the other end of the line.

"Dad?"

"Madison, I just wish you'd consider giving this cheerleading thing a rest, maybe for a little while. Focus on your schoolwork. Don't you want to have some other extracurriculars? Like voluntee—"

"Dad!" I cut him off, trying to throw the phone cord off my hand but instead almost yanking it out of the phone itself because it was so tangled in my fingers. "For the hundredth time, this is not a 'cheerleading thing.' This is my life. It's what I love to <u>do</u>. I don't know how you don't get that by now. And I do care about my schoolwork. You make me out to be some kind of delinquent. My grades are great. Besides, I do have another extracurricular—my drawing, remember?"

I think he would rather I just study and do homework 24/7. His dream must be for me to become a dowdy librarian with long braids and oversize glasses with ten cats (i.e., the opposite of Mom).

GIVE ME A
45!

"All right, honey, let's not argue." He cleared his throat. "Listen, uh, Beth is really looking forward to meeting you on Friday."

I tried to conjure up an image of what his latest girlfriend would look like. The name Beth, for some reason, makes me think of a woman in a boring dress with sensible shoes.

"Um, ok. Me too, I guess," I mumbled. "I gotta go do homework, Dad," I said, knowing this would be a perfect out. Dad just loves homework.

I could tell Mom was hovering nearby, because her blond hair kept on poking in and out of the doorway of the kitchen. She gets protective when Dad and I start fighting about cheerleading.

We said good-bye, and—surprise, surprise—a second later, Mom appeared.

"You were <u>so</u> listening in, weren't you?" I teased her.

"I certainly was not!" she said, her eyes wide with indignation. "I was merely coming downstairs to grab"—Mom looked around the kitchen—"a fresh set of hand towels from the closet."

"Mom," I pointed out, "the hand towels are in the upstairs closet."

"Oh." She smiled, flinging her blond ponytail behind her shoulder. "I guess you're right. Well, I'll just get

GIVE ME A
46!

them later!" she said brightly.

I hopped off the counter and opened the fridge.
"You're the worst liar." I assembled some leftover pasta
to take upstairs. "Mind if I just eat in my room?" I
asked.

"Be my guest," she said. Her tone was totally cool,
which I am sooo glad about. I can usually tell when Mom
is mad about stuff like that.

Anyway, today was another frustrating day of
practice. No one except Katarina—who knew them
already—was able to learn any of the simplest
sets of jumps I tried to teach. And now, after this
conversation with Dad, I just don't really feel like
getting into any of it with Mom. She's just a reminder
of everything I've worked for that I haven't gotten.

Yet.

The only thing making this day better right now?
Cold pasta. Yummy!

GIVE ME A
47!

Spirit Level:
Full of Wrath

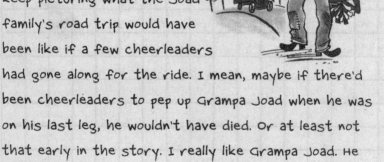

GIMME A J!

GIMME AN O!

In English we're reading
<u>The Grapes of Wrath</u>. I just
keep picturing what the Joad
family's road trip would have
been like if a few cheerleaders
had gone along for the ride. I mean, maybe if there'd
been cheerleaders to pep up Grampa Joad when he was
on his last leg, he wouldn't have died. Or at least not
that early in the story. I really like Grampa Joad. He
has spunk.

Right before English, I passed Tabitha Sue in the
halls, so we stopped to chat about practice. I guess
since I've never had to rely on her voice for any other
reason before, I've never noticed it—but her voice
is the squeakiest, shrillest voice **EVER**. It's like a
chipmunk on helium, in outer space. I mean, it's not

GIVE ME A
48!

always like that—just when she's nervous. I must make her nervous, and cheerleading must make her nervous, because in the classes we have together she's totally normal sounding.

Tabitha Sue was asking me how my morning was going, but I couldn't help but think, "How is this chipmunk-in-space voice going to make us sound during a cheer? What are the Titans going to think when they hear us? We won't even be able to do **THAT** right!" (Note to self: maybe there is something I can do to help Tabitha Sue learn how to not be so nervous?)

But I have a soft spot for Tabitha Sue. That girl has got dedication with a capital D. The Titans practically laughed her off the mat, but here she is, on the Grizzlies, with a smile on her face.

"See you at practice!" I shouted after her as she tottered down the hallway. Oh, yeah. For a cheerleader, she's also lacking this thing called "grace."

I had fifteen minutes to kill before English. I leaned against the bulletin board near my locker and wrote in my journal. I wanted to jot down some ideas I had for later. I guess I'm becoming some kind of de facto captain. Not like I should be superproud of that—who else is going to do it? Ian? Ha-ha. I also tried to keep an eye out for Bevan in case he happened to walk by.

GIVE ME A
49!

Ever since the day I almost broke my nose on him, I've been dressing a little nicer in hopes that he'll see me in the halls.

Suddenly, my journal went flying out of my hands.

"Hey, watch where you're going," Evan said in a mock bullying tone. This is one of our oldest tricks with each other.

"Er, ok," I said, trying to approximate the same baritone voice.

My journal was lying perfectly on its back, with the pages open for all the world to see. Anyone walking by could take a gander at my Top Secret page of Grizzlies uniform designs. I've been working on them since Monday night. After drooling over the Titans and their Teen Vogue-perfect uniforms, I couldn't stop thinking about how ours can use a total reboot. That is, if our school feels like coughing up some cash. (Big chance there!)

Evan's striped tie (an older-brother hand-me-down for sure) mopped the floor as he stooped down to swipe my journal.

"Lookie what we got here," he said, an amused grin on his face.

I grabbed the journal away from him. "Hands off, mister."

GIVE ME A 50!

"Ooooh, sorry. Top secret zookeeper stuff?" he said, loping after me down the hall.

"Great comeback, Comicon! By the way, nice tie." I tugged on it playfully.

"Cool, huh?" he said, holding it in front of him like it was some alien accessory. "My big bro gave it to me from his college-interview days." (I was so right.) "Oh, did you check out last night's SuperBoy?"

(sidebar: SuperBoy is this awesome blog that Evan started last year, and it actually has been getting pretty popular among the comic geeks. You could even say he has kind of a following. It's about a guy who everyone thinks has superpowers to save the planet from horrible disasters and stuff because of this one time he happened to be in the right place at the right time and he helped prevent something horrible from happening. But the truth is, he's just a regular kid. He doesn't dispute the SuperBoy rumors, because he totally enjoys the spotlight. And now people come to him for every problem—big or small. He listens to their problems, and in each story the characters think that SuperBoy

GIVE ME A 5!!

solves them. Somehow each problem resolves itself more or less, and each time they think he was the reason.)

"Sorry, E, I'll catch up on SuperBoy tonight. Hey, have you given any more thought to what we discussed? You know, turning SuperBoy into an official comic—like, a printed one?"

"No comment."

"E!" I said, giving him a little attitude.

"Let's just say I'm working on it."

"You're weird. Fine, whatever."

We reached my English class, and Evan's class was only two doors down, so he decided to hang for a bit longer and listen to some music he'd downloaded to his iPod. I saw the swish of a pleated skirt go by and looked up to see Clementine, trailed by two of the hottest guys in the school. She left this scent of lavender and jasmine behind her, and I actually saw Evan sniff the air and then look around. His eyes zoomed in on Clementine. I guess what they say about wearing a good scent is true. It really does attract men. (Not that Evan's a man, really, but you know what I mean.)

As she talked to the two guys, she sort of looked at me at one point, but only for a second. It's not like I expected her to jump out and give me a bear hug.

GIVE ME A 52!

(Ha-ha, get it?) Yeah, right. Imagine, a Titan being like, "Heeeeey, Maddy, I just love that shade of lip gloss you're wearing. Can I borrow some? Want to come over here and meet these cute guys?" I'm sure if I were a Titan, I'd be standing next to Clementine. I'd be batting my eyelashes right along with her and talking about what parties we would be going to this Friday (instead of my lame dinner with my dad). We'd probably have an intense practice later and then all go over to Katie's house—no, to Hilary's, because I heard she has this insanely huge bedroom with a walk-in closet. We'd be so exhausted from cheering our butts off all week, but then we'd make, like, amazing tacos or . . . No! We'd order in and talk about all the fun we'd have that night at the party we'd been invited to. . . .

"Um, Maddy?" Evan asked, interrupting my reverie.

"Huh?"

"Why are you staring longingly at Clementine Prescott?" Evan asked me.

"Me? What?" I asked incredulously. "I wasn't."

"Liar."

"Fine. I guess a part of me just wishes that our two teams weren't so separate, you know? Why does it have to be the Grizzles on one side and the Titans on the other? Don't we cheer for the same school?" It wasn't

GIVE ME A
53!

exactly what I'd been thinking, but as I was saying it, I realized it is something that's been bugging me lately. Or maybe I just want more reasons to be near the Titans, that's all.

Evan started to get his things together to head toward class. "It's because they're the Titans and they're 'untouchable.' Right?" Evan asked me, making quote marks around "untouchable."

I rolled my eyes and agreed with him just because I didn't feel like arguing. "Yeah, totally."

But I know it isn't true. I think people see how serious and devoted the Titans are to their team and sport and think that somehow that makes them untouchable. What people don't understand is that being on a cheerleading squad that's at such a competitive level is like being in a tight-knit family: Everyone sticks together and, well, newcomers have to prove themselves a little. But I have a feeling that once I show them what I'm made of, I can be part of that family too.

It's just taking me a little longer to get there than I imagined.

GIVE ME A
54!

After practice, home sweet home

Spirit Level:

Havin' a Spirit Attack

At practice today, Ms. Burger handed out our team schedule with the list of "games" that we will be spreading our cheer to.

She had it all typed up and printed out on her Life Studies stationery, so at the top of our Grizzly Bears games schedule were Ms. Burger's signature flower, which looked like something from a package of feminine-care products, and the words "Life Studies." Very official.

"I am pleased to formally announce that the cheer season for the Grizzly Bears is about to begin," said Ms. Burger, smiling broadly.

I don't know why a part of me was secretly hoping there'd be a soccer game (scratch that—I know why, and the answer starts with a B) or a football game or something. We all know that the Grizzlies are notorious

GIVE ME A 55!

for cheering on nerd-type games. And yet I was still surprised and bummed when the list Ms. Burger handed us read as follows (drumroll, please):

1) math league
2) Tennis
3) chem league
4) chess club
5) Bowling

Will someone **PLEASE** hand me a shovel so I can bury myself in a deep hole and never come out? Thanks. Can you believe this?!? I mean, I understand that we are a little bit cheer challenged (ok, fine, A **LOT**), but c'mon. chess? chess is a **SILENT** game! what are we supposed to do to cheer on chess!?! mime?

After Ms. Burger's announcement and some stretches to get us warmed up, Katarina and I tried to lead the team in some tumbling drills. I decided we'd start with some easy ones—or, at least, ones that **WE** thought were easy. Apparently, no one except Katarina and I seemed to know the meaning of "straight line." We had people rolling every which way all over the field. I think kindergartners could have done better.

"You have to rolling in street," Katarina said

GIVE ME A 56!

disapprovingly as she watched Ian and Matt forward roll directly into each other.

They both sat on the grass looking up at her, scratching their heads.

"Huh?" they asked simultaneously.

"Street!" she said, throwing her skinny arms straight up in the air to demonstrate. "Roll in street!"

I was only half-listening because I was working with a mess of my own: Jared and Tabitha Sue.

Next thing I knew, Ian and Matt were jogging toward Hunt's Lane, right on the outskirts of the field.

Katarina looked like smoke was about to come out of her ears. Her usually ghost white complexion was beet red.

"Where are you guys going?" shouted Ms. Burger from her usual perch in the bleachers.

"Katarina told us to roll in the street," Matt shouted back.

"I told zem, street. Zey don't listen," she said, closing her eyes and shaking her head in frustration.

I took a deep, cleansing breath.

"You guys, come back here," I shouted. "She was telling you to roll straight. It's her pronunciation. Work with us a little, please?" I pleaded.

Well, this just tickled them silly, and for the rest of practice Ian and Matt were joking about doing

GIVE ME A 57!

cartwheels in the street, doing handstands in the street, sleeping in the street—you get the picture.

By the time the sun was going down, I was pretty wiped from (a) babysitting my teammates and (b) teaching the ABCs of cheerleading to almost everyone on my team. I looked across the field at the Titans. They were practicing formations and extended stunts. Two of the Titan guys lifted one of the girls high up in the air into a bow-and-arrow pose. Their teammates clapped as she dismounted.

After everyone else went home, I practiced a heel stretch and thought about the upcoming week. The Grizzlies' first game is about a week away. It's going to be my job to figure out a routine that is simple enough for a group that collectively can't even do cartwheels. But it will still have to be good enough that it won't get back to the Titans that we aren't prepared for our first game. Man, this is gonna be tough.

At least by now they must have noticed me on the field teaching my teammates everything I know and practicing on my own. That must count for something! And when Katie, Hilary, and Clementine one day finally see that I'm the standout member of my team, I'll be plucked out of the Grizzlies in no time.

Right?

GIVE ME A 58!

On the drive home, I told Mom about our superexciting cheering schedule. She tried to give me an encouraging smile, but finally she admitted, "You're right, Madington. You can do much better than this."

I leaned back in my seat and put my hands over my forehead. "All I can think is, like, math league? I can't even imagine what kind of cheer we'd do for that. And who is even going to be watching?"

Mom pursed her lips in thought. "I guess that's what you signed up for, though. The Grizzlies have always cheered for those kinds of teams. But the point is, you're not going to be a Grizzly forever, right?"

I fiddled with the knob on the radio. It kind of annoyed me a little that she just came right out and said the obvious: that the Grizzlies are known to cheer for the loser groups at school.

"Yeah, I know," I said. "But until then, it's just kind of humiliating."

After we got me home, I figured a hot bath and catching up on SuperBoy would help my mood. There's nothing like a lavender vanilla bubble bath à la Bath & Body Works to soothe those achin' cheer bones. (When I started gymnastics, Mom introduced me to the magic of bubble baths, and

GIVE ME A 59!

the cure for a hard day's practice!

boy do those do wonders for sore muscles.) I briefly thought about taking my computer into the tub so I could enjoy two of my favorite pastimes at once. But then the thought of death by electrocution hit me, and I nixed the idea.

"Mads?" I could hear Mom's voice muffled through the bathroom door. "You gonna eat dinner with me?"

"Uh-huh, but can I have, like, ten more minutes of tub time?"

"Ok! Just wanted to know if I should set the table for two. And also, I wanted to tell you some ideas I had for your math league cheers."

"Great. Can't wait."

Ugh. Maybe I shouldn't tell her every single thought in my head about the Grizzlies. Now she is going to be all up in my grill about my problems. And of course dinner will now be all about cheer. Just when I want a tiny break from it.

I have a lot of work to do. Homework. Uniforms to design. Routines to create. A team to whip into shape. Jeez, I wish I never had to get out of the tub. . . .

GIVE ME A
60!

Friday, September 10

Post-dinner DISASTER, in bed

Spirit Level!

Desperately Seeking a Bib

It's always the nights that seem harmless that end up being the most disastrous. Mom and I were sitting on our oversize couch—the same one we've had since I was, like, a baby. I remember I used to build houses out of the big pillow cushions when I was in first grade, and then Lanes and I would pretend we were Godzilla and Bigfoot and take turns toppling them. Or sometimes we'd just use them as really good hiding places from the world.

Tonight, Mom and I were using the couch for chilling purposes before Dad picked me up for the big dinner with him and Beth. Well, actually, Mom was Googling math cheers for our first "game" on Tuesday. I'd been scribbling ideas for the past hour but couldn't think of anything remotely clever.

I'm not quite sure why I became de facto cheer

GIVE ME A
6!!

writer for our team, as well as de facto captain. But it happened like this. At practice the other day, Ms. Burger asked which of us would be writing our cheers. Jared and I raised our hands. Then, almost immediately, everyone on the team pointed at me. I felt bad about not giving anyone else a chance. But that only lasted for, like, a minute, because I realized that any cheer Jared writes will include an homage to Kristin Chenoweth in <u>Wicked</u>, or something like that.

"Hey, Mom?" I asked, glancing from the clock on the kitchen wall to my wristwatch.

"Yes, sweetie?" asked Mom, typing away.

"Do you know this clock is fifteen minutes fast?"

She tilted down the laptop screen and gave me a weary smile.

"Yep. Been meaning to change it, but you know. Life gets in the way," she singsonged.

I raised my eyebrows. (What is it that Mom does all day long besides get involved with my cheer life?) I absolutely hate having to wait any longer than necessary for Dad.

"Ooh, hon, listen to this. I think we have a winner." Mom beamed. She tilted the laptop toward me so I could see the screen.

Suddenly, synthesized piano music began playing

GIVE ME A
62!

from her laptop, and a man's voice started singing a folksy tune:

"Cosine, secant, tangent, sine,

Oh, geometry, you're so fine.

You're a trigonometric angle

And I hope someday you'll be mine."

Mom was actually grooving to this as it was playing, and I hoped she was joking, because otherwise I was ready to be like, "Ok, peace," and run screaming with open arms to Dad's car. I know it's been awhile since Mom's cheered and all, but seriously, that? If we dare do something like this at a Port Angeles school math competition, we'll be Port Angeles roadkill.

"You're not serious, right? Please tell me you're not serious?"

"Mads, c'mon. Lighten up! Of course I'm not!"

T.G. I was so relieved. Then I was frustrated.

"Ugh!" I threw my head back. "All these math cheers sound so dorky!"

"You know what this reminds me of?" Mom asked.

Usually, Mom's trips down memory lane make me feel good. But tonight, this one gave me a weird feeling in my throat. Like I wanted to just tell her to stop. I couldn't figure out why exactly. Maybe it's because I know that when Mom was a cheerleader, she

GIVE ME A 63!

would never have been caught dead at a math league tournament. But I pretended to be a good sport and listened patiently to her story anyway. This whole dinner with Dad's new girlfriend must be pretty rough on her. I figured I owe her one.

Mom closed the laptop and rested it on top of a teetering pile of newspapers and magazines on the coffee table. "We once had to cheer at this nursing home, where all the residents were participating in arts and crafts and sports, if you could call them that." Mom smiled. "You know, we did it as our cheer charity. And it was practically impossible to come up with just the right cheer and the right stunts for the day— especially since we didn't want to show off too much in front of the elderly." She laughed. "So we decided to do a whole cheer sitting down and stamping our feet, and we worked in a way for the nursing home folks to join in too!" She looked off into the distance at the spot above my head, obviously daydreaming about some memory I couldn't see. Nor did I want to. It was the stupidest story ever.

I still don't see how her story compared with mine at all. What her team had done was for CHARITY—as in, a special occasion. Our math league cheer—that is an everyday kind of thing

GIVE ME A 64!

for the Grizzlies. And the people on my team can't do stunts even if they want to. In fact, the old people's sports are probably more advanced. We're the B-team. And Mom used to be a Titan. It's not like I'm following in her footsteps. My cheer existence is all about rooting for spectacle-wearing nerds, not cute guys in helmets. (Ok, so, the Titans have the occasional old lady thrown in there too.)

I was about to say something to Mom, but I held back.

Dad finally arrived, fifteen minutes late. From what I could see of Beth, she didn't look at all how I pictured her. She actually was more the businesswoman type: suit, high heels, expensive-looking bag. Her hair looked perfectly blown out, as if she'd just gone to a salon. And her perfume nearly gagged me to death on the ride to the restaurant.

"Honey, you ok back there?" Dad asked me. "You're so quiet."

No, I was not OK. I was doing my best to conserve air. And he hangs out around this woman VOLUNTARILY?

We went to this restaurant called Le French Frog, which is one of the most expensive (aka snotty) restaurants in our town. It's known for its bad service,

GIVE ME A 65!

high prices, and really strange food. As soon as you walk in, practically every table stops what they are doing to give you a once-over. I'd never been there before, but Evan had gone once with his parents for an anniversary dinner and told me all about it. Or, rather, warned me.

Luckily, I'd had a feeling we were going to go somewhere fancy shmancy, because ever since Dad started dating again, fine dining has been his new thing. It's kind of funny, because when I was little, fine dining meant Panda Palace on Sunday nights, or ordering in from Domino's. Which was fine with me, but whatever. Must be an old-person thing.

how cute is this

I wore a supercute scoop-back dress with a raffia bow around the waist that I ordered online, and it just came in the mail yesterday (score!). Even better, the bow matched the bow on my shoes! So, luckily, when the waitstaff, busboys, and patrons were appraising my outfit, I felt confident that at least I wasn't going to be asked to leave for not being dressed properly.

Of course, the maitre d' took an extra-long time

GIVE ME A
66!

to find our name on the reservations list. Keep in mind, there were about fifteen tables there, and only three of them were occupied.

"Ah, yes," he said, feigning shock when he got to our name. Then he smiled. "Right this way. We have a special table in the corner just for you." Ha! Special. Yeah, sure buddy. You totally picked it out for us.

I think I detected some Brooklyn in his accent, which he was desperately trying to hide. (The funny thing I discovered about Le French Frog is that no one who works there is actually French.)

The three of us sat down and looked awkwardly at one another until Dad broke the ice.

"So, Beth," he said, picking up her hand. "Why don't you tell Madison a little about yourself? I really want the two of you to get to know each other."

Beth seemed a little horrified at the prospect of getting to know me, because she actually backed away a little when he said this. Really.

I quickly learned that Beth is one of those adults who cringe when they're near kids. It's like she thinks she might get pimples again if she gets too close. She has this insane ability to smile and frown at the same time. In that beginning conversation, I found out riveting tidbits of information:

GIVE ME A 67!

1) She works at a bank, doing some kind of complicated job that I pretended to understand but that sounded really boring when she described it.

2) She is from St. Louis, Missouri. Her parents currently live in a "community" in Florida. Her dad's hip isn't in good shape.

3) She likes her bread warmed. When the bread came to the table, she asked the busboy to take it back "por favor." I saw Dad blush slightly, but he didn't say anything.

4) Supposedly she speaks French.

The waiter came by to take our order. I didn't really know what much of the menu meant, but Dad insisted that Beth was a "Francophile" and that we should just let her order for all of us.

"Oh, Madison, have you ever tried foie gras?" she asked, tilting her glasses toward the bottom of her nose.

I shook my head no.

"Fabulous, you'll love it," she said to me. Before I could protest, I heard her order, "Three foie gras s'il vous plait." I wasn't so sure about this meal, but I decided to do as Mom had told me and be a team player, at least for Dad's sake.

As Beth gave the rest of the order, Dad looked at her adoringly. Blech!

GIVE ME A 68!

"So, Madison," she said to me, frowning, "enough about me. Tell me about you and this cheerleading business," she tittered.

"Well, cheerleading is, like, <u>my life</u>," I kind of snapped at her. "I'm totally obsessed with it. It's an amazing sport," I said, picking off an end of a small baguette.

"A sport?" she asked.

Dad folded his arms across his chest and leaned back in his chair, shaking his head. He knew what was coming. The cheerleading-is-a-sport speech. And I gave it to her. Soup to nuts. It just makes me so mad when people act like cheerleading is so easy—like there's no skill involved. Let me tell you something: There's skill all right. It takes strength, grace, and technique to do stunts. Beth wouldn't last one second at the top of a pyramid.

"But, Madison, don't you think there are so many extracurriculars that are better for you than cheerleading?" She took a sip of the wine that had been placed in front of her.

Was Dad, like, feeding her cue cards?

I took a deep gulp of my iced tea. "There are a lot of great extracurricular activities at school. And as cheerleaders, we support all those other activities through cheer. We get to be a part of all of them,

GIVE ME A 69!

in a way," I said. (OK, so the truth is, I've never actually thought of it that way before, but that was seriously the most genius, in-your-face answer of all time. Go, me.)

Beth pursed her lips, silently disagreeing.

The foie gras was delivered to the table, and I couldn't help but think it looked like disks of mushy cat food.

Beth took a dainty bite. "Mmm, exquisite," she said, gazing at my dad.

I decided to take one for the team and show Beth that I was no slouch in the adventurous-eating department. I can be refined, even if she thinks I'm just a stupid cheerleader. I took off a nice-size piece with my fork and put it in my mouth before I could second-guess it.

As I started chewing, however, the second thoughts started happening whether I wanted them to or not.

"Hey, um . . . what exactly is foie gras?" I said, trying to keep the food in one side of my cheek.

"Duck liver, of course," said Beth, smiling serenely at me. "A specially fattened duck."

And then I did what only came naturally after

GIVE ME A 70!

hearing that I was eating some foreign animal body part. I **SPIT** the whole huge bite back onto my plate. But because I hadn't done any advanced spit-up planning, the regurgitated food dribbled **EVERYWHERE**—on my chin, on my **DRESS**, on the table.

"Excuse me, please," I said to a horrified-looking Beth and a very angry-looking Dad.

I gunned it to the bathroom and dabbed my mouth with toilet paper. I looked down at my dress and saw ugly brown stains where I'd spit up my food. My fab new dress was an absolute mess!! (Hey, that's almost a cheer 😊)

I heard someone using the sink outside my stall. I figured whoever was out there had already witnessed my demise in the restaurant. No use waiting for them to leave the bathroom.

I walked out to the sinks with confidence. That is, until I registered Clementine Prescott smugly preening in front of the mirror. She was running a comb through her long, wavy brown hair. (The kind that stays perfect even in 100% humidity.) My jaw must have dropped to the floor in shock, because it actually kind of hurts a little. Of all the restaurants in town, Clementine Prescott just had to be at the exact one

GIVE ME A 7!!

I was in that night? Why??? Do I have a little cloud o' doom following me around wherever I go? Can I not just have one awkward night alone with my dad and his awful GF without some disaster having to be witnessed by one of my cheerleading idols, please, O Ye Gods of Cheer?

"Enjoy your appetizer?" Clementine asked, looking pointedly at my brown, smudged dress.

"Uh . . . I . . ."

I couldn't even manage a complete sentence, I was in such shock and so completely embarrassed.

I burst through the bathroom door and back into the restaurant. I couldn't help but wonder what was worse: facing the judgmental stare of Clementine or the disappointed look on my dad's face. I know what he was thinking: "Just this once, Madison, couldn't you hold it together?"

T.G. my entrée seemed to be based on a familiar part of a chicken—a simple chicken breast. No guts or liver there, phew! I let Dad and Beth do most of the talking for the rest of dinner, and I think they were ok with that. I think Beth was worried I might have another spit-up episode if I talked and chewed at the same time, so she just let me chew and didn't ask me any more questions. Dad must have made up some

GIVE ME A 72!

reason for my spitting up the foie gras besides my thinking that Beth ordered me food that looked and tasted like cat throw-up.

When I got home, it was pretty late, and I was glad to see Mom's door was closed and the pulsing blue TV-glow was coming from under it. That usually means she's sleeping and that I shouldn't bother her. I so don't feel like talking about the night, anyway. I'm always better off just writing it down, which is about all the reliving of the night's horror I can endure.

GIVE ME A
73!

Spirit Level:
Give Me an U-P-C-H-U-C-K

Today I woke up practically strangled in my
pom-pom from an absolute nightmare. Dad's
girlfriend, Beth, was dressed as a Titan (like
I said, nightmare), and she was doing all these
backflips and cartwheels as Clementine led the team
in a cheer all about what happened to me at the
restaurant last night. Can you believe it??

On Saturdays I usually lounge in bed for a while, and
then Mom and I have a late breakfast together. But
this morning I was totally freaked out by that dream,
so I decided to just come out to the backyard and
start working on some cheer moves.

It's really nice out. Perfect shorts and a long
sleeve tee weather—which is, like, my ideal fall day,
because it still feels a little bit like summer but with
a hint of what's to come. I tried to inhale all the

GIVE ME A
74!

smells of the outdoors—my neighbor's azalea bushes, the freshly mown grass, someone cooking bacon for breakfast.

But the scene from last night in the bathroom keeps replaying over and over in my head. I see Clementine's face and hear myself stammer, "Uh . . . I . . . ," and I just can't stand it. UGH.

I texted Lanie and Evan to see if maybe they'd hit the mall with me later.

Lanie: Can't. Pottery class.

Evan: Going 2 <u>Secrets of the Moth Eaters IV.</u> Sorry!

Ugh. As much as I love them, once in a while it would be nice if we could do normal friend things together, like go to the mall or see regular movies (not ones with subtitles—Lanie's fave) about regular people (not people with superpowers). Maybe even go to a regular bookstore.

But no. Lanie insists that the mall is "soulless" and that anything that isn't an independent film is just for jocks and that all chain bookstores do is "support the man." And Evan, well, he's on a perpetual quest for the most mind-blowing comic, so that pretty much eliminates most normal social venues for us.

So, on a beautiful Saturday, when people like Katie Parker and Hilary Cho are sunbathing their long, toned

GIVE ME A 75!

limbs by the pool, I'm having a boring day of practicing my around-the-world jump. But if we're being honest (and hey, this is my journal . . .), it really does need some work.

After breakfast with Mom, I started sketching some more ideas for the Grizzlies uniforms. But as I was sketching, I started to wonder—what is the point of designing a new uniform, anyway? We've been given the same hand-me-down, scratchy, flea-infested uniforms as every other Grizzly before us—so, who is going to pay for these fancy new duds?

Maybe today'll be the day I'll find out my real dad isn't this weirdo who likes bad-French-food-eating, child-hating women like Beth. Instead, he's actually this Daddy Warbucks character, and he'll be, like, crazy obsessed with cheerleading. Maybe he was even a cheerleader when he was a kid. And we'll meet and do a big cheer-slash-dance number in his huge mansion. Then I'll show him our ratty, tattered uniforms. He'll frown and snap his fingers, and a parade of maids will tap-dance down the hall holding our team's brand-spanking-new uniforms, and they'll all be MY DESIGNS!

All of a sudden I felt something wet land on my head. I touched it with my forefinger.

GIVE ME A 76!

"EWW!"

Bird poop. A bird literally **POOPED** on my dreams! Well, daydreams, but that's basically the same thing, for me anyway.  I'll take that as a sign that I have to get real. No Daddy Warbucks is going to buy us these uniforms. We'll have to buy them ourselves. Or raise the money to buy them. That's when it hit me: a fund-raiser! I had no idea what we'll do to raise funds, but I have to have enough faith in my team to know that even if we aren't the best cheerleaders, we can at least come together to raise some money. I can't wait to tell everyone on Monday at practice.

Monday. Monday means school, which means facing whatever rumor Clementine decides to spread about my chewing challenged-ness. I can just picture the rest of my life from here on out. Clementine will tell the rest of the squad how Madison Hays Likes Her Meal So Much She Eats It Twice. They'll all have a good laugh and

GIVE ME A 77!

remember that I'm the kind of girl they might want to think twice about taking out in public. Great way to convince a squad to take you onto their team, huh? And I can't even begin to imagine what Bevan Ramsey will think of me once he hears **THAT** story.

Maybe Bevan is a vegetarian! And when he hears my story, he'll think it was really sweet of me to spit up my food. "She didn't know what she was eating," he'll say after hearing Clementine's tale. "She felt bad for the poor, fat ducks, and I fully support her dedication to our animals!"

Yeah, a girl can dream. Eww, I have to get this bird poop off me, like, **NOW.**

GIVE ME A
78!

Monday, September 13
After lunch, study hall

Spirit Level:
In the Money

$$$

Mom was all about my fund-raising idea. But like all things with Mom and cheer, she's almost TOO much about it. This morning, I was trying to enjoy some perfectly good Pop-Tarts (untoasted, just how I like them) and flip through the funnies section of <u>Wake Up, Port Angeles</u>, and she threw down this forty-page printout, practically right on my plate.

"Voilà!" she said, all triumphant-like.

I looked up at her, midchew. (BTW, I've been practicing the art of chewing with my mouth clamped shut really hard, so that nothing can surprise me enough to make me spit things out.)

I swallowed my Pop-Tart. (Score!) "What's this?" I asked, curious.

"Fund-raising ideas!" she said, walking over to the coffee machine. "I scoured the web late last night,

GIVE ME A 79!

searching for new and exciting ways that cheerleaders these days are fund-raising."

I just gave her an "I'm annoyed" look.

"You know, for your uniforms," she pointed out, stirring sugar into her mug. Uh-huh, I got that, Captain Obvious.

The header on the first page of the printout read, "Top Ten Things You Can Do to Cheer on the Ca$h!" Part of me was thinking it was nice of Mom to think of me and go to the effort of helping me research fund-raising ideas. But another part of me wanted to say, "Mom, I think I can handle this part. I may not be able to do a perfect scorpion pose on the top of a pyramid, but I know how to type search words into Google. Probably better than you." But I didn't say that. I didn't say anything. But, I mean, does she think that I'm such a cheerleading failure that I don't even know how to organize my own team's fund-raiser without her help?

"What's wrong, Madington?" she asked, biting her lip. She does that when she's worried about me, which is actually a really annoying ploy, if you think about it. I know that means she's worried, which means I get guilted into not getting mad at her, because I feel bad and I know she's just trying to help. Mothers.

GIVE ME AN 80!

"Nothing," I said, packing up to head to school. I figured I'd just say thanks for her help and do this my own way anyway. Besides, I have enough to worry about today already with the whole Clementine thing. "Ready to go?"

Mom motioned to the printout on the table. "Aren't you going to take that to show it to your team?"

"Oh. Right." I was hoping she'd miss that detail. It's not like our kitchen table isn't covered in tons of other scraps of paper, magazines, and newspapers.

At school I mentioned my fund-raising idea to Jared, who is in my second-period math class with Mr. Hobart. But he got a little too excited.

"I say we do a production of Spring Awakening!" he said, flipping his long bangs back dramatically and widening his eyes. "You'd be a perfect Wendla! You're just the right size. Wendla should always be played by a petite, just like Lea Michele."

I haven't seen Spring Awakening, but Lanie has—twice. She went with her older sister when they visited an aunt in New York City. She told me it was the best musical she has ever seen in her life, and I'll take her word for it. I've only seen The Lion King and Legally Blonde.

"Um . . . let's ask everyone at practice today,"

GIVE ME AN 8!!

I said, to be fair. Thankfully, I don't think a musical fund-raiser like this will fly with the Testosterone Twins either.

Mr. Hobart has this insane ability to hear everything you're saying when you shouldn't be talking. And then, when he calls on you, he makes you repeat whatever you've just said. Today, I was his target. He cleared his throat in that really phlegmy way of his and said, "Excuse me, Miss Hays? Does your chatter mean that you would like to answer the problem on the blackboard?"

I looked up at the board, and basically, this is what I saw:

$$\sqrt{\frac{C = (\Sigma - 3674^2)\ 538.24}{Q487(\pi + a2)(x4)^{37\frac{1}{2}} - B}}$$

I must have started drooling or making that stupid noise that cartoon characters make when they don't know the answer to a question, because he finally just gave me a stern look and called on another person.

Lucky break. Except for a couple of people chuckling at my expense, but still. Could have been worse. Could have gotten detention.

At lunch I couldn't help but notice Katie Parker and her crew looking my way. I just know Clementine was

GIVE ME AN 82!

telling them about what happened at Le French Frog. I can just see it, I'll walk down the halls and forever endure taunts like, "Need a bib, Madison?"

A similar thing happened to a girl named Helen Bassett last year. She had one of those little mirrors with Lisa Frank artwork on it in her locker—you know, with the unicorns and hearts and stuff (so she was kind of asking for it). Anyway, she was scratching her nose (or so she says) when Clementine saw her and said "Gross! Helen just picked her nose!" For the rest of the year people whispered things like "Find anything good?" or rapped the words to "Gold Digger" whenever she walked by.

Anyway, this is so not the way I plan on getting the triumvirate to notice my mad cheer skillz.

"Earth to Madison," said Evan in a mock alien voice.

"Oh, sorry guys. Was just busy picturing my future at school as a Certified Loser."

"And that would be different from your current existence <u>how?</u>" Lanie said, scarfing down a french fry.

"Ooh, good one, Lanes, you got me where it stings," I said, clutching my heart.

"Ladies, ladies. I need your attention," said Evan, pushing his cafeteria tray away. He unzipped his backpack.

"After much anticipation, I would like to present to you a long-awaited work by the one and only Evan Andrews. Hot off the presses." He handed us each our own, signed copies of Superboy to the, Um, Rescue!

Lanie and I let out squeals of joy.

"Try not to fall in love with me, girls. I'm not good at time management."

"E! You did it! Wow!" I said, leafing through my copy.

"I told you I was going to. I just needed to make sure the fan base was ready for it."

The first comic already had me cracking up.

Seeing Evan's comics gave me a totally amazing idea.

"Evan, how about for the Grizzly Bear fund-raiser we sell your first issue of Superboy?"

GIVE ME AN 84!

Lanie gave me a look like, "Girl, please." I mean, I knew that this might take some major prodding. It took practically ten years to convince Evan to take his blog from web to print. I could only imagine what it would take to make him sell it to the kids in our school.

"Yeah, Mads. I love you and all, but that is definitely not happening," Evan said, snatching my copy back.

"Oh, come on," I said, taking a bunch of SuperBoy mags and fanning them out as if they were on display. "We'll set up a table at a couple of games, we'll sell them, and you will be the author signing them for fans. I'll help you run the booth, and whatever profit the team makes, you'll get a percentage."

"Mads. I only have Internet fans. They don't go to games. They play them at home, on their computers and Xboxes. Remember?"

Looking at all the work Evan had put into producing a printed comic, I was so proud of him at that moment. And for a split second, I wasn't sure if I was, like, proud of him like a big sister would be or proud like maybe I wanted to plant a big kiss on him. Like, on his lips. But thankfully the moment passed pretty quickly or I would have excused myself to go to the nurse's office to get my temperature taken.

"You don't know how great these are—you just have

GIVE ME AN 85!

to get them out there and let people see what you've been hiding. You're really talented."

Evan pushed his long hair away from his eyes, embarrassed. "Sorry, Mads. You'll have to raise money the old-fashioned way. What about a car wash or something? Don't cheerleaders, like, live for that stuff? I know I do, heh heh."

(BTW, it's really annoying when even Evan tries to be all boy-gross.)

"Lanes. Help me here, please?" I pleaded.

"It's true, Evan. I think SuperBoy speaks to a generation. You've tapped into the zeitgeist, Evan, and you don't even realize it. Keeping these comics from the public is doing a major disservice to our youth."

Ok, so, I only understood about half of what she just said, but I was convinced!

"Well, when you put it that way . . . ," said Evan.

With a little more ego stroking, Lanie and I were able to persuade Evan to at least try selling SuperBoy at one game and see what happens. Hurrah!! Victory at last!

HOMEWORK BREAK, LIVING ROOM

I pitched the idea for SuperBoy at practice, and luckily, the rest of the team likes it too. Jared volunteered to dress up as SuperBoy and talk to

GIVE ME AN 86!

fans in front of the table.

"I'm so excited!" said Jared. "It will be kind of like one of those Disney characters you see at Epcot. I can pose with the fans. Does he wear a cape? Or a leotard? I love leotards!"

"Sorry, Jared," I told him. "SuperBoy doesn't quite have that kind of fan base yet."

Jared's eyes practically started tearing up.

"But as soon as he does, the costume's yours," I reassured him. Jared's face immediately brightened.

Oh, and turns out that Tabitha Sue is a closet SuperBoy fan (shocking, I know). Katarina thought that SuperBoy was the son of Superman, and we took a few extra minutes out of practice to straighten out her misconception. Ian and Matt even promised to beat up anyone who makes fun of Jared in his costume, which I think was kind of sweet!

Ms. Burger commended me on coming up with the fund-raiser idea in the first place. She took me aside while everyone was practicing our routine for the math league tournament and said I had great leadership qualities. Now, normally, I'm not one to get all sentimental, but I have to admit it was really nice to hear. No one's ever really singled me out before like that.

GIVE ME AN 87!

I told Mom about our idea for SuperBoy when she picked me up after school.

"That's great, honey!" she said, and then paused, squinting ahead at the road like she does when she's thinking about something. "Was that something you read in my printouts? I don't remember seeing it."

"No, Mom," I said, laughing. "I thought of it on my own. I <u>am</u> capable of having an original idea every now and then," I said. The plan was to be sarcastic, but I think it came out with a bit of an edge to it. Oops.

"Oh," said Mom, "of course you are. Hey, did you come up with a cheer yet for the math league meet?"

"Sort of." I sighed, throwing my head back against the seat. "And it is awful!"

One idea that the team came up with is a cheer about the quadratic formula, where every word is matched to another pose, but it still seems kind of cheesy.

"Maybe we can kick around some ideas after dinner?" she suggested.

"Actually, can we just have a cheer-free night tonight?" I asked.

Thankfully, she didn't argue. Lately, Mom is driving me C—R—A—Z—Y . . . what's that spell? AHHHH!!! Obviously, I love cheer and it's totally my life, but

GIVE ME AN 88!

sometimes even cheerleaders need a break, you know? I think I'm just going to relax, put cheer out of my mind, and do a little bit of drawing instead. There's this killer idea I have for a dress that might maybe possibly someday be something I'll want to wear to a school dance with a certain someone. I mean, that's clearly a total fantasy that will never come true, but hey, as I always say, a girl can dream, right?

PS—Oh! I almost forgot! Praise the cheer gods—**NO ONE** mentioned anything about what happened at Le French Frog. Crisis averted. Woot! Woot! But I guess you can never be too sure with someone like Clementine. Maybe she's just holding this juicy bit of info about me for blackmail. At least I'm in the cheer for now.

I mean, clear.

GIVE ME AN 89!

Tuesday, September 14

After math league, locker room

Spirit Level!

Brrr! It's Cold in Here. There Must Be Calculus in the Atmosphere!

We had our first game today, if you could call it that. See, Port Angeles believes every school activity has the right to—no, **DESERVES**—some level of cheer, and math league is no exception. Thank goodness, because without this policy, we Grizzlies wouldn't exist. Now, we aren't about to cheer in a classic, adrenaline-fueled gym or on the seasoned grounds of a football field with the bright lights beating down on us. Nope. Not us Grizzlies. We cheer in fluorescent-lighted classrooms—with the same graffiti-inscribed desks that spend the school day taunting us. Instead of coaches sitting on the sidelines, we have teachers. Grading students. At **MATH**.

Still, it didn't matter. We were all excited and even a little nervous. Our first game! Poor Tabitha Sue was sweating bullets. Katarina and I fought over the one mirror in the locker room that doesn't make people look

GIVE ME A 90!

like circus freaks. I made sure there were no bumps in my ponytail.

"Hey, Katarina?" I called. "Maybe you might want to, uh, tone down the makeup a little? I think you look great without it." Katarina had this full arsenal of makeup out. She'd gone from looking about twelve years old to thirty in ten minutes. Maybe she's more Titan material than I am. They always doll up before games.

(Note to self: To play the part, you have to look the part. Perhaps a trip to Mom's bathroom is in order. . . .)

glam!

Katarina gave my face a look that made me feel like perhaps I should consider a trip to the MAC counter. "Vat you are choosing to make to your face is your business. I like my face much more beautiful zen yours," she said, resuming her application of deep red lipstick.

I decided to butt out at that point. Though I really hope something was lost in translation or else I'll be very offended.

blech.

At five minutes to "game time," the Grizzlies filtered into Room 303,

GIVE ME A 9!!

where the tournament was held. "Tabitha Sue," said Katarina, "you are looking like sveat. Here, you must be of use to my towel."

Tabitha Sue smiled and took Katarina's towel. She was well accustomed to Katarina's "beautiful" way with language by now, a little more so than I am. "Thanks, Kat," said Tabitha Sue gratefully.

The math leaguers looked a little annoyed at having cheerleaders in the room, even though our sole purpose was to be **SUPPORTIVE** and **BRING CHEER** and **PEP** to their otherwise boring competition.

Two scrawny-looking guys wearing nearly identical, too-tight argyle sweaters cowered in fear as soon as they saw Ian and Matt enter the room. They **LITERALLY** shrank back and brought their arms over their heads.

"Hey, Matt, what did you two do to those guys?" I asked.

"Oh, those little dudes?" A look of pride washed over Matt's face briefly. "Hey, Ian, check it out. It's Thing One and Thing Two." He pointed at the two nerds across the room, who were now whispering to each other and pointing in our direction.

"We <u>might</u> have hidden their clothes while they were showering after gym one time," said Ian, stroking an

GIVE ME A 92!

imaginary beard. "And they <u>might</u> have had to walk back through the gym naked to find a teacher to open the lost-and-found box for them so they'd have something to wear." He laughed nastily.

After a few minutes, it became obvious that the nerds were no longer cowering in fear but pointing at Ian and Matt and laughing. Like, full-on cracking up, buckling over in their seats. People were staring. It took me a moment to realize why.

"Hey, nice outfits!" said the brown-haired nerd, motioning at Ian and Matt's cheerleading attire.

I guess at first Thing One and Thing Two—I mean, the two little guys—thought the Twins were coming in to rough them around again. And in the middle of their math tournament, no less! But then, when they realized that Ian and Matt were cheerleaders, man oh man, I can only imagine the satisfaction they felt.

Matt and Ian were a little slower on the uptake. Almost in unison, they looked down at their white sneakers, their pleated, fitted, high-waisted, pants, and their shirts with the gold tassels on them. The nerds had a point. There was no bigger **FAIL** in school than a football jock becoming a cheerleader. Especially when it wasn't even by his own choice.

"That's it. I'm outta here," said Matt, under his breath.

GIVE ME A 93!

"Me too," said Ian. "Let's bounce."

They began to shove their way past a group of students from the rival school that had just walked in.

"Hey! Get your butts back here!" I shouted over the chatter of students and teachers filling out papers and forms. I caught up to the two of them and started tugging on their shirts. Yeah, good luck to me, single-handedly trying to drag two guys who were each twice my size.

Jared, Tabitha Sue, Ms. Burger, and Katarina were looking on at our scene with puzzled expressions.

"You can't leave now," I pleaded. "Who else is going to say 'Yeah, yeah,' in our 'Let's Get Quadratic' cheer?"

"And you're the bases in the pyramid, remember?" Tabitha Sue pointed out in her chipmunk voice. (Apparently, yelling at jocks makes her nervous.) "No one else on the team is strong enough," she said drearily.

At first, neither of them seemed like they were going to give in. But then Matt looked at Ian and shrugged. "Fine. We'll do it for you guys. But if one of those science experiments over there starts messing with me, he's going down. Ok?"

"Deal," I said, hoping that the nerds kept their comments to themselves.

Unfortunately, our first performance as a team

GIVE ME A
94!

was . . . What's the word I'm looking for? Oh, right . . . abysmal. It didn't help matters that the other school's math league team didn't have a cheer squad, so we stood out—but in a bad way. Maybe it was because it is a little awkward trying to motivate people while they're scribbling away at intense-looking math problems. We might as well have been yelling, "Write harder! Write faster! Gooooo, calculators!" Ultimately, I think we were more distracting than supportive.

What was even **MORE** embarrassing was that our formations were totally off. Tabitha Sue, who was in the front row, was supposed to be kneeling, but she stood instead. I tried to make the whole team stand so that she didn't look bad, but by that time Tabitha Sue realized what she'd done and started to kneel. Then we all looked like idiots. (Big surprise there ☺)

Ian and Matt dropped Katarina during her pyramid. **DROPPED** her! And she's, like, five pounds! (T.G. no one in the room spoke Russian, because she let out a cacophony of curse words on her way down.) Miracle of miracles, they were able to handle Tabitha Sue's pyramid just fine. But Jared was over the top as usual. When he forgot some of the moves during our "Port Angeles is Mathtastic" cheer, he decided to do an exuberant macarena to kill time. With

GIVE ME A 95!

exaggerated hip thrusts. No joke.

Even worse, a Titan who I usually see at practice stopped by to give her brother who's in math league moral support. She stood by the door to Room 303 for about twenty minutes and saw most of our routine. I can only imagine what a joke we must have looked like to her. Scratch that. I don't have to imagine it. I was there. UGH.

On a good note (the ONLY good note), Lanie and Evan set up a SuperBoy stand outside the room. It was our first stint at fund-raising for the team. It was really cool that they did that for us—even though they're not even Grizzlies. (Well, they ARE getting a percentage of sales, but still.) In between cheers, Ms. Burger was totally fine with me sitting at the stand and acting as treasurer. Mom helped too—she made a huge sign of the SuperBoy cover for us and met up with Evan and Lanie right before the meet to set it up. It looked really professional. At first I was a little annoyed that she'd gone to all that trouble without consulting me first. I never would have asked her to do that for the team. But then I thought it was kind of nice and it looked awesome. Evan sold out of the whole stash that he had brought with him!

GIVE ME A 96!

And later I was like, "Duh, of course!" How did we not guess that math league would be the perfect place to start selling SuperBoy comics? The geeks are his supreme fan base! And now Evan has a list of e-mail addresses from people who want their SuperBoy as soon as it comes out—we even have fans from the other school now. Yippers! This actually might work! Now let's see if we can sell SuperBoy at, say, a swim meet. . . .

GIVE ME A 97!

Spirit Level!

No Way!

Hey, Hey! Am I Adopted? Please. Say. NO WAY!

Dad called tonight. All of a sudden he's way interested in my cheerleading. At first I heard Mom answer the phone downstairs and say, "Oh hi, Steven," and I thought she'd do the usual drill: call for me, linger nearby so she could listen in, you know. But actually, she **TALKED** to him for a bit. About what, you ask? About me and my cheerleading! And I was like, hello! Since when did this become, like, the topic of the ten o'clock news?

So I did my best impression of Lara Croft and crept down the stairs as stealthily as possible. I had a great image in my head of myself in an awesome

GIVE ME A 98!

Lara Croft-inspired unitard. One day, when I have my own fashion line, I'll have to design something like that.

As I tapped my foot ever so lightly on the second-to-last stair, I thought I'd almost given myself away, but Mom didn't seem to notice. She was standing in the kitchen with her back to me, running her hand through her just-stepped-out-of-a-salon hair and balancing on her dainty little toes like a ballerina en pointe. (PS—Who just stands around like that?)

Eavesdropping isn't normally my thing, but I firmly believe that when the topic of the conversation (me) and the eavesdropper in question (me) are one and the same, they cancel each other out, no harm done.

At one point I heard Mom's voice get all snappy, and she was like, "No, Steven, they're called the Grizzlies, not the Geek Squad. And they're just a little rough around the edges. But they are certainly not geeks. In fact, they have a lot of heart."

Ok, Eww #1: I knew Dad didn't like that I was cheering, but I didn't know he had a problem with me being a Grizzly Bear! So now he thinks I'm a giant dorko. Awesome. Eww #2: "A lot of heart?" Somehow, hearing Mom defend our "ungeekiness" left a bad taste in my mouth. I mean, I know she was only trying to help,

GIVE ME A 99!

but hearing her say that just really annoyed me.

I quietly slid down to the floor outside the kitchen so I could listen through the wall. Here's the deal, plain and simple: Mom was a Titan cheerleader. She always has been and always will be. But the question is, IF Mom and I had gone to school at the same time and her jock boyfriend had made fun of a Grizzly Bear cheerleader, would she have taken that cheerleader by the hand and said to her boyfriend, "You don't understand. They're <u>so</u> not geeks. They're just like us but with less practice." Answer: DON'T THINK SO.

When I heard her walking toward the stairs, I got off the floor.

"Honey, it's your dad!" Mom shouted in the direction of my bedroom.

"I'm right here," I said in a normal speaking voice.

"Oh," said Mom, jumping back a little, surprised.

I yanked the phone out of her hands.

"Hey, Dad."

Dad apologized for getting angry at Le French Frog last Friday, which I must admit makes me a little bit happy. He said he understood why I'd been grossed out by the food and said he shouldn't have taken his "embarrassment at the situation" out on me. That still kinda sounds like he's embarrassed by me, but

GIVE ME A 100!

honestly, at this point, whatever.

"Next time, I won't make you suffer through eating something you don't like. You can order for yourself, ok, honey?"

"Yeah, that sounds good. I'm sorry I made such a scene, though."

"I understand. I'm not really a fan of the foie myself."

"Really?" I asked.

"Hey, dating is like <u>Survivor</u>. You have to eat some nasty things in order to impress the judges."

"Ok, Dad, whatever."

Eww #3: Dad talking to me about dating is, like, the most disturbing thing **EVER**. Please, please, please make him stop!! (**BUT**, note to self: When (if) I ever start dating and it starts to feel like I'm trapped on a desert island with strangers who are trying to make me eat supergross things, then I'll consider living as an old maid forever.)

I soon realized that, unfortunately, Dad also had another reason for calling.

"Beth wanted to know if you knew her friend Irene's daughter, Ramona Bowens. I think she's in your class."

I opened the pantry cabinet to see if we had any gummy worms. We did—eureka!

GIVE ME A 10!!

"Yeah, I know her," I said, popping a gummy worm in my mouth. "She's a year younger than me. Total Model UN devotee." (Also, one of the most boring, predictable, goody-two-shoes girls in our grade. She's, like, one of those young geniuses who skipped a grade and takes all honors classes, goes to computer school on weekends, AND takes summer classes. Excuse me while I go throw up.) "Why?"

Dad laughed. "Beth thought that maybe you should talk to Ramona. Invite her over sometime?"

I spit out the gummy worm midchew (which is when it occurred to me that maybe I do have a chewing/swallowing problem??!). But this flavor was seriously gross. When did candymakers start allowing such disgusting flavors? But back to my point: Who is Beth to suggest that I throw out years of dance, gymnastics, and tumbling so I can moan on endlessly about global warming and the oil crisis??? No, thanks. I mean, I care about that stuff, but not enough to devote, like, five hours after school to it. Who does he think I am? Does my dad not know me at all?

"Uh, Dad, I'm happy with my current crew of friends, thanks."

"I'm not saying you should be her best friend, Madison. I'm just trying to encourage other

GIVE ME A 102!

interests. That's all," he said.

"All right, Dad. I'll, um, think about Model UN."
Yeah, I'll think about it in my **NIGHTMARES**.
I immediately pictured Beth sitting right next to
him, smiling encouragingly as he called his wayward
daughter (me) and told me about her amazing idea to
get me off the cheer train.

Dad and I had an awkward good-bye. I'm sort of
beginning to feel like a stranger in my own family.

Update: The gummy worm was just a root-beer-
flavored one (blech). The rest of the bag was
completely delish!

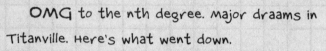

Wednesday, September 15

After practice, locker room

Spirit Level!

Give me an O-M-G

OMG to the nth degree. Major draams in
Titanville. Here's what went down.

I showed up early to cheer practice and saw that
the Triumvirate (Katie, Clementine, and Hilary) was
also gathered in the gym, on the opposite side from
where we Grizzlies usually hang. Lately, the Titans had
still been out practicing near the sports field, while
Ms. Burger had moved us indoors. (Jared had been
complaining of fall allergies.) I thought something was
up when I saw those girls, but I didn't think much of it
until the rest of the Titans started filtering in.

Then, a little while later, Jacqueline Sawyer came in,
looking pretty confused and a little p'd off.

She marched up to Katie, who was doing her lunges
with those long, perfect legs of hers. "Um, Katie?"
Jacqui asked, tapping on Katie's shoulder. "When did you

GIVE ME A
104!

all decide to move practice to the gym? And why didn't anyone tell me? I've been standing out there like a loser for a half hour."

At first Katie didn't look up from her stretch. You could tell she felt totally awkward, because for once she didn't have this smooth look on her face. This was a first for Katie, or at least in my experience of watching her. (I'm not a stalker, it's part of my training! Promise!) Then she stood up to face Jacqui. "Actually, Jacqui, you won't be needed today."

Gasps all around the room. Or maybe it was just me gasping very, very loudly.

"Wh—what do you mean? I'm the top flyer in the routine for next week's game," said Jacqui defensively. And then she started getting angry. She did the whole eyes-getting-narrow, voice-getting-lower, hands-on-hips thing. "Did you replace me for next week's game without telling me? This is so not fair, Katie. We always talk about switching flyers out as a team."

Katie grabbed Jacqui's hand and took a step back as if to pull her away to tell her privately what she wanted to say. But Clementine beat her to it. "Jacqui, this isn't just about switching you out for a game. You won't be needed today or any day. You're off the team."

Jacqui was so shocked at first, it took her a

GIVE ME A 105!

couple of moments to respond. "Excuse me?" she asked, almost in a whisper. She looked around at the other cheerleaders as if perhaps Katie and Clementine had gone crazy. "Off the team? What's that supposed to mean?"

"It means," Clementine said with a smile, "that we know about your little problem." Clementine mimed throwing back pills.

Hilary laughed at Clementine's mime.

"Hilary, stop," snapped Katie.

"Seriously, I have no idea what you guys are talking about," Jacqui said, taking a few steps back in protest.

Katie looked almost sad. "We were going to talk to you, but . . ."

"Look, we found the pills you were trying to hide in your gym bag, and we looked them up online. You need professional help, Jacqui," said Clementine gravely. "And we can't have a teammate who's on steroids. We'll totally get disqualified from Nationals."

There were murmurs all around the team. Apparently, Katie, Clementine, and Hilary hadn't told the rest of the team their reason for eliminating Jacqui until now.

All of a sudden Jacqui burst out laughing.

"See? It's serious, guys," said Hilary, pointing to Jacqui. "Look at her!"

GIVE ME A 106!

"No!" said Jacqui, clutching her stomach. "I'm laughing because you guys are idiots! I don't know if you have problems searching or reading—or both. But the pills you found in my bag are a prescription from my doctor for a pulled muscle. If you had read the label correctly, you would have known that. I can even have my doctor call Coach Whipley."

Oddly enough, I realized that Coach Whipley happened to not be at practice that day. Surely she would have defused the situation a bit, right?

"Clementine, you really looked it up, right?" Katie hissed at Clementine.

Clementine appeared slightly unsure. "Yeah, I'm pretty sure I typed it in the right way."

"Hey, Jacqs, let's talk about this after practice, ok?" said Katie with a friendly smile. "If what you're saying is true, then of course you're back on the team. We just need to talk it through and make sure our facts are all straight so we're not putting the team in danger of disqualification."

Jacqui stood there with her arms crossed. "Wow, that's really big of you, Katie. But don't you think you should have gotten your facts straight <u>before</u> kicking me off?" she barked. "You know what? If this is what being a team means to you, then I don't want any part

GIVE ME A 107!

of it. No, thanks." Jacqui turned on her heel and walked away, her sneakers squeaking noisily on the gym floor.

Clementine made the "loonie" motion with her hand, spinning her finger around her ear, but Katie slapped her hand to stop her.

"Ow!"

"Don't be immature," Katie scolded her.

I couldn't believe Jacqui stormed out on the Titans like that. Obviously, it had all been a misunderstanding. She's worked so hard to be on that team—and she was one of the best members of the squad! The Titans were her life. No one on that team can do the stunts she can do. She was the best flyer they had. And yeah, Katie totally should have gotten her facts right first, but she was clearly just looking out for her team. It wasn't the way I would have handled it, but I understand where Katie was coming from—if she truly thought Jacqui was taking steroids. It's the most serious offense when it comes to cheerleading. Your team can go from Nationals-bound to disqualified in a nanosecond—not to mention how serious it is if one of your teammates is caught up in something like that.

This was bad.

It was really hard to concentrate on my own practice after that. I couldn't stop thinking about

GIVE ME A 108!

how shocked Jacqui looked when she heard she'd been booted from the team. At least we didn't have that kind of drama on the Grizzlies. The most I have to worry about is whether Ian and Matt will pummel each other to death before the upcoming tennis match.

Totally wrong to say (I mean, wrong to say in public, but this IS my journal), but maybe the Titans will be looking for a replacement ☺?

PRE-DINNER UPDATE, MY ROOM

Ok, embarrassing much? I was buckling up in Mom's car after practice when Bevan walked by with his soccer friends. He looked soooo cute in his cleats and socks! (IF worn by the right person, the right way, socks CAN be cute.) He was walking toward the car, and for a split second I considered saying to Mom, "Step on it please!" because I wasn't sure if I should, like, wave or smile or just totally ignore him. But the sight of him left me kind of paralyzed, so instead I just sat there, staring at him like an idiot. At the last second before we drove away, his eyes locked with mine, and I think I detected the tiniest smile. I almost got hiccups, I was so excited.

Then IT happened.

"Honey, do you want to stop and say hi to your

GIVE ME A 109!

friends?" asked Mom, blatantly pointing to Bevan and his buddies like they were animals at the zoo.

"Ohmigod, Mom, stop pointing! No! Just drive!" I said. I quickly tried to compress myself into the foot area of the passenger seat, blushing furiously. To the average passerby it must have looked like one moment, Mom had a passenger, the next, just a backpack.

So embarrassing. Whatever romantic moment we had shared was shattered, I know it! I'm certain he now thinks I said to my mom, "Hey, look! There's that cute boy Bevan Ramsey from my class!"

How loser-y can you get? You'd think I'd have this down by now. What are the chances the Grizzlies are rubbing off on me??

GIVE ME A 110!

the coolest!

Monday, September 20

After practice, bleachers

Spirit Level:

P-S-Y-C-H-E-D. What's That Spell? Psyched!

Maybe I should have seen this coming, but Jacqui started hanging out around the bleachers during our practices after she left the Titans. At first I was like, "Hey, she's coming to check out some of our stellar moves!" Yeah, right. But then I thought, "Maybe she's up to something."

Which is much more like the Jacqui Sawyer I know.

Sure enough, after practice today, she came up to me while I was about to practice some advanced tumbling that the rest of my team isn't ready for.

"You're not that bad, you know," she said, standing over me on the practice mat as I recovered from a particularly bad back walkover.

I quickly stretched and got up off the mat. "Oh, thanks."

"I don't think the Grizzlies have ever had a

GIVE ME A
!!!!

cheerleader like you on their team," she continued.

I practically flipped out (to myself, of course, not in front of Jacqui) because I couldn't believe someone of Titan caliber was commenting on my skillz. I mean, I know I'm a pretty good cheerleader, but I've never gotten noticed by a Titan or, um, an ex-Titan. Unless I count my mom, which I don't.

"Thanks, um, again," I said, suddenly feeling self-conscious. I did a quick instant replay in my head of that day's practice and hoped that the team didn't do anything too embarrassing. We walked toward the bleachers together and sat on the lowest ones, by the basketball net.

"I know it might sound totally out there, but what would you think if I said I wanted to join your team?" she asked. She actually looked pretty vulnerable at that moment. For Jacqui, anyway.

This time, I was really floored. Jacqueline Sawyer, an actual Titan cheerleader, wants to join OUR team? She left the best team in all of Port Angeles pretty much on purpose—hey, they offered her a position back—to become a lowly Grizzly?

"Hey, Madison. Hello?" I think I must have looked at her like she was speaking an alien language, because she started waving her hand in front of my face.

GIVE ME A
112!

"I don't get it," I said. "Why would you want to be a Grizzly? You're, like, one of the best Titan cheerleaders in the school."

Jacqui laughed. "You mean <u>was</u> one of the best Titan cheerleaders. You must have gotten the memo that I left: Good news travels fast here."

"Yeah," I said, looking down at my palms. "I know."

"So, will you have me? On your team?" she was looking at me expectantly for an answer.

A picture began to unfold before me of what the rest of cheer season would be like with Jacqui on the team, and **IT WAS BEAUTIFUL!** I'll have a buddy after practice to work on advanced cheer stunts with. Together, we can teach the rest of the team a couple more interesting and cool looking stunts. Maybe the two of us can even do a real routine together—possibly even with Katarina! I've always wanted to do a superintense routine that starts out with, like, something mellow from Muse and then builds up into a set of Black Eyed Peas and M.I.A. remixes. With Jacqui's help I can probably even learn how to perfect my scorpion!

"Yes! Ohmigod! Yes, we'd love to have you on the team!" I almost hugged her—I was that excited—but restrained myself. I can't wait to tell Mom and Lanie

GIVE ME A
113!

the news!!! With Jacqui's help, the Grizzlies are actually going to be legit. And quite possibly, so am I.

BTW, we sold more SuperBoys at this week's tennis match—which goes to show that SuperBoy has more than just nerd appeal. Yay! And in even better news, no one (read: Katarina) got dropped on her butt this time during our routines. Double yay!

Lanie just sat there looking resolute. "Whatevs. They snubbed my bestie. And you're an amazing cheerleader. So, that's what I think."

Lanie was propped up on her twin bed, where I had a view of the new piece of art she has hanging on the wall behind her.

"What I think, dear Lanes, is that the poster over your bed is C-R-E-E-P-Y. How do you sleep at night?"

The poster is of a big-eyed girl in an alley. The girl's eyes looked like they might swallow her whole face.

"It's by an artist named Keane. I'm collecting him now—or, um, reproductions. Isn't it awesome? I got it in the mail today."

"Yeah, awesome. And now you have a creepy, dead-looking girl over your bed who looks like she might kill you in your sleep. And you think I have problems?"

"OK, Mads, if I don't get any sleep tonight, I'm

GIVE ME A 116!

Monday, September 20

Nighttime, Under the covers

Spirit Level:

Shakin' in My Uniform

Just got off video chat with Lanes to tell her about Jacqui joining the team. She didn't freak out like I did. I get it—it's not like Lanie is Miss Cheer (far from it)—but she was all like, "That's cool," and I was like, "No, it's amazing!" And she was like, "Yeah, it's nice," and I was like, "Lanes! It's ridiculous!"

"Fine, I'm just gonna say it. She's a Titan. And during tryouts, she didn't go out of her way to rally for you to be on her team."

Awww. Lanes is the best BFF a girl can have. Holding a grudge against the entire Titan team because they didn't take me on this year. . . . Now, that's BFF dedication right there.

"Lanie, it wasn't up to her. It was really Clementine, Katie, and Hilary's call. Jacqui was up there, but she wasn't part of the Royal Triumvirate, as you call them."

GIVE ME A 115!

blaming you." She pointed at her screen.

   We signed off and I climbed into bed, thinking about what Lanie had said. I didn't really think for a second to be mad at Jacqui just for being a Titan. I've already accepted that I didn't make the team. And with her help, hopefully, I'll be a Titan in no time. Maybe Lanie is just worried I'll be spending time with a Titan—someone I look up to a lot. But she has no reason to be worried. Lanes is my best friend. She'll get over it eventually . . . right?

Get this: Today we had the best practice **EVER**, all thanks to Jacqui. She kept the whole team on its toes, because she has a little bit of a drill sergeant thing about her, and also, she has Titans experience. First she led us through a nasty session of deep stretches we'd never done before. The Testosterone Twins were moaning in pain, but they didn't dare disobey her, because if they did, she'd give them fifty push-ups as punishment.

It was a bit of a mess, but everyone was excited to be shaken up a bit by someone with that much training. Now that Jacqui has joined the team, the two of us are more like co-captains, which is fine with me. She can obviously teach us all a lot. Everyone was sweaty and out of breath by the end of practice, but psyched. We

GIVE ME A 118!

could all tell we are on our way to improving.

Jacqui sat down next to me on the gym floor to stretch as everyone else gathered their things to leave.

"That was awesome," I told her, giving her a high-five.

"Yeah, well, I've been dying to kick Matt's and Ian's butts since I started watching your practices," she said, with a mischievous gleam in her eye.

"Ohmigod, me too," I said, smiling. "But I never figured out how to do it. Who knew that making them touch their toes to the back of their heads would be worse than a noogie?"

"Every bully has a weakness," said Jacqui knowingly. "So, that Burger lady—what's her deal?" Jacqui asked.

"Oh, she's just, like, our chaperone. We don't have a real coach. We're kinda like the redheaded stepchildren of the school compared with the Titans. Um, I thought you knew that," I said, surprised.

"I don't know. I guess I never really thought about it," said Jacqui, frowning. "I've always been more about cheering and not really into the drama of it. Until now, I guess. I hate that everyone knows my business. It's, like, the talk of the school."

"Yeah, I know. It sucks," I said, thinking of what almost happened to me with the thing at Le French

GIVE ME A 119!

Frog. "Gossip spreads like fire here," I said, giving myself a good neck stretch. "But it kind of seems to me like it was all a big misunderstanding," I continued. "Do you think maybe if you and Katie sat down and talked, they'd take you back on the team?" I couldn't believe I'd just said that, because today had been so great. But I still couldn't imagine Jacqui not on the Titan squad.

"Are you kidding?" Jacqui said, staring me straight in the eye. "No way would I go back to those backstabbers. I'm going to make them regret losing me to the Grizzlies. And you are going to help me."

"Me?" I asked, shocked. I'm the last person who wants to get on Clementine's or Hilary's bad side. No, thanks, none for me, please. "I, uh," I stammered.

"Just think of it as a way for both of us to get what we want. I'm going to help you bring the Grizzlies to the next level—like you never would have imagined."

"Is that humanly possible?" I asked. I tried to picture what Tabitha Sue's "next level" would be. Not turning left when she's supposed to turn right? Not constantly coming to practice with the back of her skirt tucked into her underwear?

"The team just needs to be pushed a little harder, but I think we have potential," she said, as if she were

GIVE ME A 120!

planning the ascension of the Grizzly Bears in her head at that exact moment. "The Grizzlies are going to blow everyone away this year, and with you and me together, we'll make it happen."

"So, what is it that you'll get out of it?" I asked tentatively.

"Me? Well, the Titans hate to see other cheerleaders succeed. It will make them really peeved to see the Grizzlies get good. Really good. And it will just make them even more mad that they doubted me with the whole drug thing."

I was thinking, "I'll believe this whole Grizzlies Being Awesome Cheerleaders thing when I see it," but instead I just nodded. "Ok. Deal. I'm down with making the Grizzlies a great team. That's been my goal since the first day."

"Awesome," said Jacqui, reaching her hand out for a shake. "In that case, I was wondering," she continued, "what if we had a real coach? Like, someone who actually knew what they were doing? Didn't your mom go to the National Cheer Association championships as, like, the youngest Titan cheerleader ever?"

The idea of my mom being my coach was about as obvious to me as putting ketchup on an ice-cream sundae. Or wearing skinny jeans to practice. (Actually,

GIVE ME A
12!!

I'm pretty sure Hilary did that once. And somehow, miraculously, she succeeded in not ripping her pants. But man, that must have hurt!) But once Jacqui got going with this idea, she wouldn't stop.

Skinny-jeans toe touch

"Yeah, but Jacqui, that was, like, decades ago," I said, feeling all sorts of weird.

"Ohmigod, this would be perfect! You have to ask your mom to be our coach!" Jacqui said, launching into a brief cheer. She jumped up and put her arms into a V, and then clapped. Whoa. She really is a born-and-bred cheerleader.

Jacqui put her hands on my shoulders and made me face her. "Do you want the Grizzles to be stuck in Loserville forever, or do you want them to finally be taken seriously? I've seen how seriously you take this team. You're fund-raising, for goodness' sake. The last Grizzly fund-raiser was, what, in 1970? Come on, you're either going to go all the way or not at all. And if you're going all the way, you need a coach. Not a 'faculty adviser,'" she said, making quote marks in the air.

GIVE ME A 122!

She must have seen in my face that I was caving, because she jumped cheerleader high (which is about five feet higher than the average person) and booked it to the locker rooms to make her announcement. "Wait!" I shouted after her. "I need to ask her first!"

She didn't seem to care or even to hear me. I saw her run into the boys' locker room first, from which I immediately heard shouts of "Yeah! Hot coach!" and "Awwwright" like Quagmire from <u>Family Guy</u>. Then she skidded into the girls' locker room, and I can only imagine what the scene was like in there.

Oh, brother. I mean, mother.

Thursday, September 23

Morning, study hall

Spirit Level!

Hit by the Bang Bang Choo Choo Train

Mom came to the end of practice yesterday to officially accept the position of coach and talk to us about our goals for the year and how things are going to work and stuff.

I could totally tell that Ms. Burger was relieved someone else would be taking over the actual coaching duties of her so-called job, so that she could truly zone out during practice and fully commit to her latest hobby: LOLcats—those pictures of cats with funny, misspelled captions next to them.

I'm kind of happy that

I IZ A CAT
lol

GIVE ME A
124!

she's moved on from the bridge desk calendars. But
the thing is, lately she's been printing out her favorite
pictures and captions from those LOLcat websites
and bringing them to practice. "Aren't they a hoot?"
she always asks. She's even trying to put together a
trip to an LOLcat convention with her fan friends and
mentioned that if anyone from the team wanted to join,
she'd talk to our parents. (BTW, that is sooooo much
worse than a comic-book convention.) So, on second
thought, I think I liked it better when she kept her
interests more to herself.

Anyway, the point is, the Mommy madness has
officially begun. Since the moment we asked Mom to be
coach, she's been fluttering around the house like a
loonie, singing old cheers and waving her pom-poms like
mad. She's coming to practice today (yikes) for the
first time and couldn't be more excited. Last night, I
caught her in her bedroom trying on old cheerleading
outfits. From, like, when she was my age. The scary
thing is, the outfits fit! It's like she's stopped aging
or something weird. She didn't know I was watching,
but she started doing this cute little cheer, and
her arabesque was flawless (of course). I couldn't
remember the last time I'd seen her flex her cheer
muscles. She's always so busy encouraging mine.

GIVE ME A
125!

At breakfast this morning she was busily searching the web for "appropriate coaching outfits," as she called them.

"Mom, you can just wear, like, normal gym clothes. You don't need to turn this into a whole shopping spree."

"I want to look the part. I'm doing this for real now, Mads," she said, typing away. "I'm not just driving you to and from cheer camp."

"So, what am I supposed to call you, Coach or Mom?" I asked her as I bit into my Pop-Tart.

"Coach, of course," said Mom, squinting at the computer. "You don't want the other kids to think I'll be treating you differently. Because I won't be, Madington. I'll be pushing you just as hard, if not harder."

"Um, Mom, pushing me harder than the other kids would be treating me differently," I reminded her.

"Oh. I guess you're right." She focused her sea-foam eyes onto mine. "Fine, then I will push everyone as hard as I push you. Good?" she asked cheerily.

"Great," I said with mock cheer, giving her two thumbs up.

At school, Lanie, Evan, and I met up at the "Lounge" before first period.

"Can't get enough of your mom at home, huh? You just have to bring her to school, too?" asked Lanie.

GIVE ME A 126!

"Yes, that's exactly why," I quipped.

I told them about practice the other day and how the whole thing happened with Jacqui bringing up Mom being our coach, in gory detail.

"Man, that's rough," said Lanie, twisting her finger through a pigtail. "But knowing you, you'll figure out a way to find the positive in it. Besides, you and your mom are, like, this close?" she said, crossing her index and middle finger.

"Yeah," I said. "I know. I love my mom. And she's definitely a lot cooler than most moms. But lately, she's getting more involved in my cheer stuff than I need her to be."

"Wow," said Evan, wiping fake tears away from his cheeks. "Our little Maddy, growing up." He patted my head affectionately.

"Oh, come on. Would you want your mom to suddenly be, like, your boss at the comic book store?"

Evan wrinkled his nose. "You know my mom hates comics. If she sees them lying anywhere outside my room, she considers them trash and throws them out. So, that's an irrational question."

I sighed. "Whatever. I guess in the long run having her as coach will be good for the team."

"Speaking of the team," said Evan, grabbing his

GIVE ME A 127!

backpack off the floor, "I have some new SuperBoy stuff to show you guys."

He handed us each copies of unfinished scenes from the next SuperBoy.

"Just some sketches. Nothing final, but I thought you'd like to see the work in progress."

"Cheerleaders this time, huh?" asked Lanie.

I looked down at the comic she was referring to. It seemed to be about some cheerleaders who beg SuperBoy to take them all to the dance because their dates have been held hostage by an evildoer.

"Thought I'd cater to the fans," he said, brushing imaginary lint off his shoulders.

"Oh, ok, EgoBoy," I said, kicking him lightly.

"I'm just being honest," he said, his voice cracking a little, like it always does when he tries to act macho.

I did happen to notice that one cheerleader in particular looks a lot like me. She was wearing a Grizzly uniform, had my long, wavy hair and freckles, and was small like me. I was going to tease him about it, but then something in me made me change the subject. "Just make sure you bring enough copies tomorrow night, ok?"

Since the tennis match, everyone has been asking about SuperBoy. Evan has even gotten approached a

GIVE ME A 128!

couple of times in the halls. Lanie and Evan are planning to set up one of their SuperBoy stands at the Titans' big Friday night soccer game. It could potentially be the biggest SuperBoy sale yet. In the meantime, we've asked everyone on the Grizzlies to add SuperBoy to their blogs and e-mail signatures. The whole team has also been passing out flyers with samples of the comic in class and advertising the upcoming sales of SuperBoy at tomorrow's game. I'm superexcited.

We talked about our game plan for the next night.

"The Grizzlies are all going to take turns manning the stand with you guys," I told Evan and Lanie. "I'll be there the whole time, obviously. Unless Mom makes me focus on watching the Titans in all their glorious perfection."

"What do you mean?" asked Evan.

"Oh, well, as coach she's already declared that she will be making us watch as many Titan home games as possible. She said that to learn from the best, we need to watch the best. First thing on her agenda is watching their old videos at practice."

"Ooh, I'll bring the popcorn!" Lanie joked, rubbing her hands together in mock anticipation.

"Feel free. But another one of Coach's new rules is superhealthy eating during cheer season. So unless it's

GIVE ME A 129!

all-natural, no butter, kettle-popped popcorn, you'll be having my portion."

"Bummer," said Evan.

"Guess we'll just have to figure out a way to sneak you some contraband popcorn," said Lanie, packing up her stuff to get to class.

Ok, so in first-period history class, I tried to imagine what practice is actually going to be like later. Will I really be able to call Mom "coach," or am I going to say "Mom" first? Will it bother my teammates that she's my mom? Probably not—they freaked out when they heard she was going to be our new coach. I hope she knows how much work she's got cut out for her. It's not like an ordinary cheerleading squad. She's probably thinking we're like the Bad News Bears and she's coming in to snap her fingers and whip us into gorgeous, amazing, cheerleaders. Boy, is she in for a surprise. Maybe she'll just throw her hands up in despair after one practice. And then what will we do? That would be an awful blow to the team morale!!

I was on the verge of a panic attack when something in my brain was like, "Madison. Take a giant chill pill. It's not prescribed by a doctor, but don't worry. It won't get you booted off the Grizzlies."

I'm probably getting all worked up over nothing.

GIVE ME A
130!

Friday, September 24
Nightime, bed

Spirit Level: YeaH!!
Turnin' Up the Heat

First a brief update on the team: Yesterday's
practice with our new coach (ha-ha) was good! (I know,
huge surprise.) Mom took over in a really good way. No
one seemed upset that I was the coach's daughter, so
that was a huge relief. And Mom came to practice with a
set idea of what we would do that afternoon. she let
Jacqui lead the stretches, and then we had a really
similar practice to what I've seen the Titans do. I was
like, "Hey, Mom, couldn't you have told me your trade
secrets before?" We felt like a real cheerleading squad.
Even though, of course, most of the team had A LOT
of difficulty doing the things Mom wanted them to do.
But it was cool—she was really helpful, trying to show
them how to do new positions and stuff like that. And, of
course, Jacqui and I weren't too shabby as co-captains,
assisting her ☺.

GIVE ME A
13!!

In other news, this I Heart Bevan thing has just reached a whole new level of pathetic. Tonight at the game, when I was **SUPPOSED** to be helping out with the SuperBoy fund-raiser, and when I was **SUPPOSED** to be watching the Titans and taking notes on their every move, I did something else entirely: I stared, slack jawed and completely mesmerized by the perfection that is Bevan Ramsey. How I never noticed him until he collided with our cheer pyramid and then my nose is beyond me, but a part of me is wondering if this is fate.

He is totally one of the best soccer players on his team. Scratch that—in all of Port Angeles. His whole team practically worships him, and so does the rest of the school. I noticed a bunch of other girls around me going all gaga eyed whenever he scored a goal or rescued the ball close to the outfield. Which brings me to my problem: Since he is such a sports god, with everyone vying for his attention, how in the world will I ever get him to pay attention to me?

Solution: the best way I know how—**CHEER!** First for the Grizzlies. Then, after they see how awesome I am—for the Titans, and then I'll just cheer for Bevan. ☺

Here's a little ditty that crawled into my head when it was my turn at the SuperBoy booth. If anyone reads

GIVE ME A
132!

this, though, I swear I will probably never be allowed to cheer in this country again.

Hey, hey Bevan

You make me sigh

Don't say no

You'll make me cry

Hey, hey Bevan

You make me feel like heaven

Call me: 555-2247

Ok, who am I kidding?! That cheer is totally going to get me booted into a foreign country. (But if it's someplace like England or Ireland, it'll be ok, because at least there they speak my language.)

Anyway, I think Lanie and Evan were annoyed with me tonight. It might have been because I wasn't paying attention AT ALL when people were handing me their cashola.

"Um. Ring, ring? Ring, ring?" said Lanie.

"What?" I said, flustered. I released my gaze from the soccer field and realized there was a line of people waiting for SuperBoy comics. From me.

"You're supposed to be ringing people up, remember?"

"Oh. Right," I said, quickly taking a ten from a pixie-ish upperclassman in cutoff shorts and a sailor top. "Sorry."

GIVE ME A 133!

"It's like you've totally checked out or something," said Evan, his brow furrowing disapprovingly. "We've been talking to you for the past five minutes, and you've just been responding in 'mmmmmsssss.'"

I blushed. Was it that bad?

"Why don't you just go back to the bleachers," said Evan. "Tell Jared he can start his shift earlier."

"I'm sorry, guys. I'm just, like, a space cadet today. I'm ready to concentrate now."

"It's cool. Just, like, come back later when you're feeling it," said Evan, not looking me in the eye.

I could tell by the sound of Evan's voice that he was hurt but he didn't feel like arguing.

I walked back to where the Grizzlies sat with Mom (I mean, coach ☺) on the bleachers. They'd been the first to show at the game and scooped up front-row seats (the better to watch the amazing Titans). Also, Mom said it's important for us to support all the school teams, even when we aren't cheering at those particular games. Talk about school spirit overkill. No wonder Mom cheered all through high school.

"Awesome! Front-row view of the Titans!" exclaimed Ian, high-fiving Matt. Their faces were practically on level with three Titan girls' skirts—and the girls were about to start cheering.

GIVE ME A 134!

Tabitha Sue rolled her eyes. "You guys are so immature."

My thoughts exactly.

Mom had told us to bring notebooks so we could note our favorite formations and stunts. That way, we could each "work toward obtaining different goals" for ourselves during the season. (A part of me thinks she just wanted an excuse to watch her alma mater and relive her glory days.)

I took out my notebook but had trouble putting anything on paper. Well, anything related to cheer. Because even though one of my fave things in the entire world is watching great cheer routines (and believe me, the Titans are up there), I still couldn't stop staring at Bevan: Bevan and his perfect calves running up and down the field . . . Bevan nonchalantly whipping his head to toss his sweaty hair out of his face . . . Bevan taking a sip of Red Bull. Now, **THAT** I had no trouble sketching at all!

GIVE ME A 135!

"Wow, Madison," Mom whispered to me, "you are so focused on the field today. I love it!" She rubbed her hands together in excitement. "It makes me so proud to see you following my suggestions so closely." She smiled.

I quickly covered my notebook with my body. "Uh, yeah," I said brightly.

Little did she know the source of my "focus" had nothing to do with cheer.

One person, however, was not fooled at all. Jacqui switched seats with Katarina and leaned in close to me. "If you know what's good for you, you'll stay away."

Cryptic much?

"What? Why?" I replied. "What are you talking about?"

"He's really cute, that's a given," she said, nodding in the direction of my new love, who was about to score yet another goal. "But something you might not be aware of? He and Katie Parker used to date. But he broke up with her this summer for reasons she wouldn't ever tell us about. And ever since, she has declared him an archenemy of the Titan cheerleaders.

GIVE ME A 136!

we weren't even allowed to say his name in a cheer," said Jacqui.

Wow. I couldn't imagine someone as perfect as Katie Parker ever getting dumped. The idea made me feel a little sorry for her. Also, how did I **NOT** know who Katie Parker was dating? It's, like, my job to know all these details as, like, part of my Titan-to-be training. Way to drop the ball, Mads. . . .

"You're kidding. Just my luck."

"I wish I was," she said, rolling her eyes. "I mean, who bans an entire team from speaking one person's name? I think it's insane, if you ask me. But she did it. You can't even say his name in passing. As in, 'And then the teacher asked Matt, Bevan, and me to go to the back of the room.' Big no-no. She'd make you get to the top of a pyramid and have you dropped."

"Katie wouldn't do that," I said, laughing.

"Don't laugh! It's not funny. And you have no idea. That's what she does to a team member who dares speak his name. Imagine what she'd do to a non-team member purposely trying to date him," she said pointedly.

"Jacqui," I said, lowering my voice so she'd know to do the same, "in case you haven't noticed, I'm kind of what you'd call invisible to guys like Bevan. You weren't there, but the only reason we've even met before

GIVE ME A 137!

is that he literally ran into my pyramid. Ran into it. Because he didn't even <u>see</u> me there!"

"Ok, whatever. Just letting you know, is all," said Jacqui, shrugging her shoulders and dropping the subject.

I guess I'm glad she warned me. Jacqui is hard to read—I can't really tell yet if she likes me or if she's merely putting up with me because I'm the only decent cheerleader on our team. Either way, it was cool of her to give me a heads-up about Bevan and Katie.

We decided to stop gossiping and join the rest of the squad and cheer for the players. Mom got a little too much into the game for my taste. She was hooting and hollering with the best of them, and it was kind of embarrassing. But it could be worse, I guess. She could be like all of those moms who go to games parading around in their daughters' juniors-size clothes, hoping that the gym teachers will notice them.

But I'm still going to have to talk to her about bringing it down a notch. I can't have my mom "bringing it" more than me.

GIVE ME A 138!

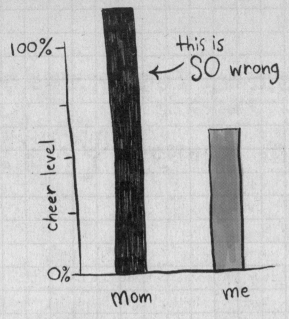

The great news? After all the sales tonight of SuperBoy, plus the previous sales, we've now made enough money for new uniforms!!! Rawk on. I promised the team that next week I would do a big reveal of the sketches I've been working on. Hope everyone likes them!

GIVE ME A
139!

spirit level: YAY!
Flying High

I don't care if I look like a dork right now, scribbling away in my journal outside the caf, but this is practically Twitter-worthy news! I was just thinking about the rumored pop quiz we are supposed to be having on quotes from <u>Romeo and Juliet</u> when I heard someone call my name. I turned around and, hark, 'twas Katie Parker.

"Hey, Madison, you got a sec?" she asked sweetly.

I looked behind me to see if there might be another Madison she could have been addressing. I wasn't used to Katie uttering my name in the school halls (or anywhere), let alone looking at me. Clementine and Hilary were on either side of her, each with one arm on a hip. After giving them both dismissive glances, she broke free from their protective barrier to approach me.

"The Titans have a favor to ask," she said, without

GIVE ME A 140!

apology. "I'm assuming you're kind of like the co-captain, right?" she smacked her perfectly lip-glossed lips together and tapped her foot as she waited for my answer.

"Well, y-yes," I stammered. I have enough good sense to know not to bring up Jacqui's name to Katie Parker.

"Good. So, here's our problem," she said, widening her eyes. "The Titans have a competition the same day as the next soccer game. And there's no way we can leave the guys without a cheer squad. Our school would look like total losers." she said the word "loser" like she had just vomited a little in her mouth.

Clementine and Hilary nodded grimly behind her.

"Ok . . . ," I said, starting to get the picture but still not quite believing my ears.

"We know the Grizzlies still need a lot of work. But maybe you can put something together that you know the team can do easily?"

I waited a few beats to process this. Katie Parker wanted MY team to take over the Titans' place and cheer on the boys' soccer team? As in, an ACTUAL sports team? Not the debate team, the chess club, the Irish club, or any of those other sports that people don't really come out to watch? One in which "headgear"

GIVE ME A 141!

means a protective helmet worn to prevent a sports injury, not an orthodontic appliance? How about . . . YES, PLEASE!!!

"Absolutely! We'd love to!" I squeaked. I couldn't contain my excitement, and I didn't really care. This will be our moment to really show everyone what we're made of. And we've improved a lot lately—especially with Jacqui on the team and Mom as coach.

"Cool," said Katie, looking back at her friends. "Then it's a deal. Just make sure you don't mess this up for us. Even though you're the Grizzlies, if you're cheering in our place, you're representing the Titans. Remember that," she said, before spinning on her pink Cons and walking away. As if on cue, Hilary and Clementine waited a beat before making an about-face and following on her heels. Their little cheerleader skirts bounced from side to side in synchronicity, causing a minor traffic collision of guys in the hallway. Boys. Such animals.

As for me, I am floating as I write this. I can't wait to tell the team! They are going to flip out. Tabitha Sue will surely scream in another range that possibly only

GIVE ME A
142!

dogs will hear. Katarina will yell with joy in her mother tongue, and Jared will probably perform an impromptu performance from Rock of Ages (not like he ever needs a reason). And Mom, well, Mom is probably going to design some kind of cheer boot camp to whip us into high gear for our first REAL game of the season. Let the fun times begin.

And you know what else? The soccer game will be the perfect time to reveal to the world the Grizzly Bears' new and improved uniforms. Awesome!

Wait! Soccer. Soccer. . . . I know someone who plays on the soccer team, and his name starts with a B. Great, now I think I might throw up. What if Bevan thinks we suck? I mean, we do kind of suck, so I guess that's not a shocker. But what if he thinks I suck? I'm not sure if I'm excited about this whole thing now or dreading this. But I guess I don't have time to ponder it too much at the moment, because the bell just rang. It's time for that pop quiz!

GIVE ME A 143!

Friday, October 1

After practice, locker rooms

Spirit Level!

Middle of the Pyramid

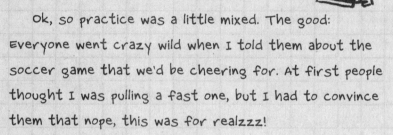

Ok, so practice was a little mixed. The good:
Everyone went crazy wild when I told them about the
soccer game that we'd be cheering for. At first people
thought I was pulling a fast one, but I had to convince
them that nope, this was for realzzz!

"Madison, if you're messing with us, you're going to
pay big-time," said Jared. He had one finger pointed at
me, and his eyes were all squinty. He was serious.

"Or what, Jared?" asked Tabitha Sue. "You're gonna
make her listen to your imitation of Justin Bieber's
'Favorite Girl'?"

Jared glared at her.

"I swear, I'm telling the truth. We are
definitely cheering in place of the Titans at the
next soccer game. I swear on our ugly uniforms,
even." I made a solemn face and put my hand over

GIVE ME A
144!

the tiny rip on my right shoulder.

"She must be seriousness," said Katarina, pointing to me.

"Holy Mother of Cheer," said Jared. "It's true!"

And then everybody screamed and hugged for, like, five minutes.

The bad: When Mom heard the Big News, she got this wild look in her eyes that said "Crazy Coach Carolyn mode," and I heard her mention something to Ms. Burger about how she might need an office so she could come in during the day to plan formations in advance of practice and stuff. Hello? Crazyville? I know she wants to kick our butts extra hard to get us in gear for the game, but seriously, an office is really taking it to another level. What would she be doing in there all day? Researching new ways to torture us?

It's one thing to have your mom on school grounds for practice and stuff. That's bad enough. It's another for your mom to be there DURING school hours. Like, what would it be like to walk down the halls and see Mom by the water fountain? I really hope that

Hey, Mom, what's uh... shakin'?

Not much, Madington. Oh honey, brush your hair. It looks a bit messy!

GIVE ME A 145!

this is either a passing whim of hers or that there isn't another office available for her to use. I'm going to have to talk to her. Oh, dread.

The team love love **LOVED** my uniform sketches, though, so that put the day back on track. Jared was a little upset that the uniforms don't include any glitter or rhinestones, but I had to explain that there's nothing glittery about Grizzlies.

Jacqui volunteered to submit the designs and order

GIVE ME A 146!

form to the uniform-making company, because she used to be in charge of that stuff for the Titans and knows her way around the website. Nice!

After practice, Jacqui and I hung around as usual to practice some more advanced cheer stuff. I've almost got my scorpion down perfectly now, and today she taught me how to get my legs perfectly straight in my heel stretch to bow and arrow.

"Hey, Jacqui, before we put the order through for the uniforms, maybe we should go to a fabric store and select exact color swatches so we can give the company references?" I asked her as we packed up for the night.

"Oh, yeah, I totally didn't think of that!" she said. "Good idea."

"What are you doing tomorrow?" I asked.

"I'm babysitting early in the morning, but I'll be free at noon. Let's meet at Sew What at, like, twelve fifteen?"

"Awesome, it's a plan," I told her.

If there's anything I love as much as cheerleading, it's fashion design. And I A—D—O—R—E going to craft stores. I have a secret obsession with the fabric and pattern department, of course. Every time I touch a new piece of supersoft cotton or a fab swatch of

GIVE ME A 147!

denim, I am immediately filled with a dozen ideas of what I could transform it into. If only I had, like, twelve more hours in the day . . . which is why I'm so happy I can at least sketch all my ideas down even if I can't actually make all of them. It will be **COMPLETELY RAD** to see one of my ideas—this new uniform—made into something my teammates and I are going to wear for everyone at school to see! Woo hoo!!

AFTER DINNER, MY ROOM

Back at home, during dinner, I asked Mom if she was really serious about getting an office at school. She looked down at her plate of grilled chicken and steamed broccoli (T.G. I'd snuck in some Doritos earlier or I'd be staaarving) and chewed thoughtfully. (Note to self: Mom doesn't seem to have that pesky spitting-out-food-when-caught-by-surprise problem. I must have gotten it from Dad.)

"I thought it would be a good way for me to become a serious part of the squad," she said. "This way, I can interact more with the kids on the team and connect with them during the day. Like the other coaches at school." She paused and looked at me, her fork poised mid-bite. "Why? Do you not like the idea?"

I didn't really know how to tell her that my reason

GIVE ME A 148!

for not wanting her to have an office isn't really about her connecting with the team at all. I know it is selfish of me to just want to be left alone during the day. So I tried to just reason with her.

"But Mom, most coaches have offices because they're part of the faculty anyway. It's not so they can connect with students."

"I know," she said. "But that's what gives me—and the Grizzlies—a disadvantage. And I think the Grizzlies have enough disadvantages as it is."

Ok, so she has a point. Anything to help the Grizzlies usually is a good idea.

But what about me? Can't Mom see my side? How would she have felt at my age if her mom had wanted to help coach her cheer squad and be at school all the time? Oh. Right. She was a Titan. She never would have been in this situation at my age. She was born a winner and has never known, even for a second, what it's like to cheer on the losing squad.

GIVE ME A
149!

Ok, so Lanie isn't doing jumping jacks over the fact that Jacqui and I have been hanging out together. Should I have expected her to, though? She was kind of weirded out by the whole Jacqui thing from the start.

"We're just going into town," I said into the speaker of my iPhone. I was in my room, still trying to decide between my thermal long-sleeved tee with the cherries on it and skinny jeans with ballet flats, or a flannel button-down and cutoff shorts with ankle boots. "We're not, like, getting married. Besides, aren't you busy taking tai chi or something this afternoon?"

"It's Krav Maga," said Lanie, haughtily. "For your information, it's a hand-to-hand combat course. Way more intense than tai chi."

"Well, whatever," I said. "You're too busy to help me pick the perfect color for our new uniforms anyway.

GIVE ME A 150!

But if you were free, I would have loved for you to come." It was the truth. Anytime Lanie is down to go to a regular store is a miracle as far as I'm concerned. But I wasn't sure Lanes and Jacqui would have gotten along so great, what with Lanes's attitude and Jacqui being all, well, Jacqui. Oh, and Lanie's latest thing is that Jacqui is using the Grizzlies to get back at the Titans in this Uma Thurman in <u>Kill Bill</u> way.

"Just be careful with that girl. She's got a nasty plan for each one of those cheerleaders, I swear. You'll see. I've seen the look in her eye at practice. Why do you think I hang out on the bleachers after school? I'm here for you, Mads."

"Lanie, that's sweet. But you need to get out more."

"I do get out, Madison Hays. I am learning the Israeli art of hand-to-hand combat." Lanie sighed. "Fine, go on. Buy fabric swatches, but I want you to text me as soon as you're back and show me what you picked out. I'm not used to being the Other Woman," she said dramatically.

"Ok, Lanes," I giggled.

When I got to the entrance of Sew What, Jacqui was there holding a Starbucks venti chai. She looked like she'd even dressed up a little for our outing. At school she's usually more laid-back in her own tomboy

GIVE ME A 151!

style—which is unusual for a Titan. By code, the whole squad pretty much looks perfectly primped and girlie all the time. They wear the latest trends as dictated by Teen Vogue, their hair always looks like it's never heard the word "frizz," and a lack of lip gloss is equal to a fashion emergency. Jacqui, however, never really seemed to get down with the rest of the squad on the primping and fashion front. Surprisingly, the Triumvirate didn't make a big deal about it. (Or, at least, I'd never heard that it was a problem.) But today she was wearing whitewashed ripped jeans with a vintage-looking belt and a fitted paisley blouse. Her dark curls hung in loose waves around her shoulders.

"Hey, did you get dressed up just for the grannies at Sew What?" I asked when I got closer.

"Ha-ha," she muttered, kicking me with her ultracute pair of clogs. "I like to put in a little effort on weekends, ok? Everyone at school kind of sucks, but you never know who you might meet around town," she said coyly, taking a sip of her chai.

"Very true," I said, silently congratulating myself on choosing my flannel-and-shorts ensemble. This seemed just the right look next to Jacqui's outfit.

It was funny, I was actually a little nervous about us hanging out. I'd gotten so used to being with Jacqui

GIVE ME A
152!

at practice and stuff, but we'd never, like, chilled outside of cheer before today.

The fabric store was pretty crowded for Saturday at noon. We had to fight our way through a throng of old ladies arguing with a frazzled-looking salesperson over the price of a bolt of Christmas fabric for their annual Christmas quilt-off. One of the elderly women—the leader of the group—was holding open the local paper to the salesperson's face to show where she had circled the 10% off coupon in bright red marker.

"Young lady," said the group's leader, using her walker to get up even closer to the salesperson. "I've been coming to this store for forty years. And every year, we get the same discount on the holiday fabric. What makes you think this year is any different?"

"I understand, ma'am," said the salesperson, her voice shaking a little. I don't think she expected her day at the sew what to be quite so dramatic. "But as

GIVE ME A 153!

far as I know, the new policy says that the discount doesn't apply to holiday fabrics."

The elderly woman adjusted her glasses to the bridge of her nose so she could glare at the salesperson. "New policy. Oh, really? I don't believe it says anything about a new policy anywhere on this here piece of paper," she said, stabbing at the paper with her forefinger. "I can still read the fine print!"

The salesperson took the paper from her and took a long look at it. "Um. Uh. Hm." She scratched her head. "You know, I think I <u>will</u> need to talk to my manager." She darted away toward the back of the store.

"That's a good girl," said the woman, repositioning her glasses and putting her hands on her hips. She looked back at her now-adoring crowd, who smiled and gave her pats on the back.

"Wow, those ladies mean business," said Jacqui under her breath.

"Remind you of anyone we know?" I asked as we continued down the aisle.

"Lemme guess. . . . Katie, Clementine, and Hilary: the Golden Years?" Jacqui laughed.

We found the apparel fabrics and located the reds, whites, and blues. It wasn't easy finding the perfect red. Lots of reds had kind of an orange hue to them,

GIVE ME A 154!

and some even looked a little pink or a little purple. Finally, we found the perfect colors and purchased the smallest amount so we could tell the company that would make our uniforms exactly what we wanted them to use.

We decided that all our hard work deserved a little treat, so we grabbed some fro-yo up the street. It was actually nice, because we didn't talk about cheerleading for a change. I found out that one of Jacqui's other great loves in life is hip-hop dance. She's been taking classes since she was five.

"I never would have pegged you for a hip-hop dancer," I admitted.

"Yeah?" she said, taking a big lick of her peanut-butter-and-chocolate-swirl cone. "A lot of people say that."

"I guess I don't really know what a hip-hop dancer is supposed to look like. I suppose maybe they'd have to, like, swagger?"

"Oh, you mean like this?" said Jacqui, doing a bouncy walk down the sidewalk to a hip-hop beat and slouching her shoulders.

"I think you have to lose the ice-cream cone for that to be effective," I told her.

"You might have a point," she said, laughing.

GIVE ME A
155!

We had a really good time the rest of the afternoon just walking around town and talking. By the time Mom picked me up, I couldn't believe we'd spent so many hours together not doing anything cheer related. I didn't really know Jacqui had a goofy side until today. It's pretty cool. Of course, if I even suggest to Lanie that Jacqui's cool and that we had so much fun today, she'll probably just say I hallucinated the whole thing. Or she'll get really mad. I think I'll just keep this to myself for now.

GIVE ME A 156!

Thursday, October 14
Pregame, locker rooms

Spirit Level!
Grizzlies Rawk!

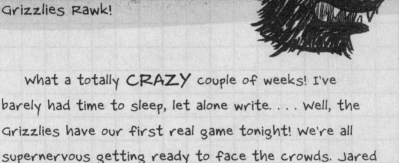

What a totally **CRAZY** couple of weeks! I've barely had time to sleep, let alone write. . . . Well, the Grizzlies have our first real game tonight! We're all supernervous getting ready to face the crowds. Jared even had a near panic attack.

"No crying in the boys' locker room!" shouted Ian as he pushed Jared into the entrance to the girls' locker room.

Ian and Matt aren't exactly the nurturing types.

"You . . . guys . . . I'm . . . freaking . . . out. . . ." wheezed Jared, completely unaware that there were half-naked girls all around him.

"Ohmigod, Jared, what's wrong?" Tabitha Sue said, running over to him in a sports bra and shorts. She quickly launched into Nurse Tabitha Sue mode. "Quick, someone get a hot towel!"

GIVE ME A 157!

"No!" Jared protested. "You'll ruin my makeup!"

"Makeup?" we all asked, turning to look at him at the same time.

"Yes," he said, patting his forehead delicately with the towel Tabitha Sue handed him. "It's important for the crowds to be able to see one's expressions from afar. Theater 101. Hello?"

Tabitha Sue, Jacqui, and I looked at one another and shrugged. We each shared a little of my Cherry Bomb lip gloss (which I totally heart), and I'm wearing my mascara from this morning. As usual, Katarina looks like she's ready to walk the red carpet . . . like, at the circus. "I think our routine is what's supposed to help us get noticed from afar, Jared," I pointed out.

"We're Grizzlies, Madison. We need every bit of help we can get," said Jared.

"He's right," said Jacqui. "The Titans always get all dolled up before a game. When Titans get ready, there's usually enough hairspray in these locker rooms to damage the ozone layer in one sitting. But we all have to be comfortable. To each her—or his—own, right?"

"Right!" everyone agreed enthusiastically. Jared still has on some blush, and Katarina has her "full face" on, as my mom would say.

GIVE ME A
158!

Even still, I'm beginning to wonder if maybe we should start putting a little more effort into getting ready for games. Especially for this one—the one that counts. I looked down at my chipped nail polish and my totes-in-need-of-a-pedi feet. But it's a little too late now. The good news is that Jared has definitely started to calm down through lecturing us on our pregame makeup application. Sweet!

Mom came into the locker room a few minutes ago wearing a red, white, and blue tracksuit. Underneath, she's wearing a T-shirt that said, "Wimps lift weights. Cheerleaders lift people." OMG. I can tell she got her hair done while we were at school today. Her ponytail is even more perfect than usual. Her makeup is flawless. She looks like a college cheerleader dressing up as a mom. (Well, at least someone on our team will look perfectly cheertastic.)

"Hey, Coach Carolyn, nice outfit!" said Jacqui, smirking.

"Mom, what are you . . ."

"You like it?" she beamed, smoothing her palms against the creases on the front of the pants. "I got it special just for today! I thought it would really

GIVE ME A 159!

tie us together as a team. Now I match your uniforms!"

Oh, BTW, our uniforms came in this morning, and they are UH.MAY.ZING. The colors are perfect, and they fit each of us perfectly. I can't believe that we actually pulled this off. I'm so proud to be premiering our brand-new look at a real game. I also can't wait for Bevan to see how cute I look in a uniform that isn't covered in sweat stains and moth holes or stretched out in all the wrong places. (That is, if he notices me, period.) Here's what my masterpiece looks like: ⟶

Brand Spankin' NEW UNIFORMS!

I rolled my eyes and looked at Jacqui, who gave me a knowing look. At least Jacqui can see Mom has gone a little overboard. But I can also tell Mom is a little nervous. This will be the first time her coaching skills will be reflected for Port Angeles to witness.

"Now, ladies," she said, looking at us überseriously. I half expected her to get down on her haunches like one of those TV coaches and start pulling out a chart

GIVE ME A
160!

with different moves that we should pull to fake out the other team. "You guys are going to do great today. I just know it! I can't wait to see you out there. I'll be cheering the loudest."

"Actually, Coach," said Jared, putting his arms around Katarina and Tabitha Sue. "We'll be cheering the loudest!"

"Oh, Jared!" said Mom, surprised. "I didn't realize you were in here!"

Ok, this is it—the moment we've been waiting for. . . . Please, o ye Gods of Cheer, let us not suck!

TIME TO PASS OUT, CASA DEL HAYS

It's a miracle! The Grizzlies actually rocked the game tonight—and it feels incredible! We went onto the field and took our places on the first set of bleachers, bracing ourselves for some boos. Surprisingly, no one booed—or threw eggs or dog biscuits at us! (That's a victory in itself!) We all looked at each other with relief and waited for the boys' soccer team to run onto the field. I couldn't wait to see Bevan in his cute little shorts and cleats (and socks ☺).

As soon as both the teams entered the field, we jumped up and did our "Get Started" cheer.

The girls shouted, "Are you ready to get started?"

GIVE ME A 16!!

two times and the boys responded, "Yes we are! Yes we are!" and then together we all shouted, "I said S, S-T, S-T-A-R-T! Start!" And we jumped up and down like maniacs shaking our pom-poms. Katarina did some backflips across our cheer line. The crowd applauded, and then we sat back down.

We were psyched. . . . It was a strong beginning to the game. We felt like cheerleaders for realzzz!

By halftime our team was winning, and we were gearing up to do a halftime performance. I was so nervous, I felt like I was going to throw up. I looked up at the bleachers and saw Lanie and Evan each giving me thumbs-up and smiling.

"All right, guys, you ready?"

"Go, Grizzlies!" said Mom.

We ran out to the middle of the field and assumed our formations. I tried not to think about the fact that Bevan was watching, or I knew I'd trip up. Jacqui led the routine, and T.G. we put Tabitha Sue in the back, because she was up to her old tricks of dancing to the beat of her own drum. Luckily, no one seemed to notice, because people applauded throughout our whole performance. Ian and Matt tried the toe touch we'd been practicing for the past two weeks, instead of opting for the easier jump Jacqui had taught them

GIVE ME A
162!

as an alternative. For the finale, Matt and I lifted Jacqui into a beautiful pyramid, where she posed in her trademark scorpion. Everyone hooted, and some people yelled out, "Go, Jacqui!" which made me feel really good for her. Ever since the incident with the Titans, everyone's been gossiping about her.

Our team won, which made the night even more amazing. And afterward, everyone came up to tell us how cool our uniforms looked. I tried to look for Bevan, but he'd already disappeared into the crowd of his grass-stained and sweaty teammates.

Mom was in hypercheer mode, so she took the whole team out for dinner at Steak & Fries—a typical postgame hangout. I kind of wouldn't have minded celebrating our first real game without her around, which I know is totally cruel, since she's part of the reason we were so successful tonight. It's just, once in a while I'd like to be a normal kid who gets to hang out with her teammates without Mother Dearest breathing down my neck. But since she was treating the team, and since she is our coach, I couldn't really tell her to go home. It also was a superspecial occasion for her to be giving the team permission to pig out ☺.

Within two seconds of entering Steak & Fries, you feel like you're coated in an inch of grease. I noted

GIVE ME A
163!

that our brand-new uniforms will definitely need a solid wash to get the smell of fries and hamburgers out of them. Too bad. The colors are just so perfect before the first washing. I saw a couple of BFFs of the Titans in the booth right behind us chowing down on grilled cheese sandwiches and salads. They paused to give our team a once-over as we walked by.

"I'm so proud of you guys!" Mom said as we all slid into an extralarge booth in the back. "And, Madison, those uniforms are the talk of the town."

Jacqui sat across from me, and Lanie and Evan sat on either side of me. They're considered honorary "spirit members" because they're the reason we were able to afford the new uniforms. Secretly, I hoped that this would be a good opportunity for them to get to know Jacqui a little better.

"You guys really were great today," said Lanie, grabbing a napkin from the dispenser. "Jacqui, that last thing you did at the end rocked."

"Yeah, that was awesome," said Evan, looking up from the oversize menu.

The waitress came over to take our order, and to our surprise, Mom ordered nachos with the works, chicken fingers, and fries three ways (a Steak & Fries specialty) for the table. In my life, I don't think I've

GIVE ME A 164!

ever seen Mom eat a nacho. She must have really been feeling good about tonight.

"Hey, Madison," said Ian from across the table. "I have to hand it to you. I don't feel like a sissy in this uniform at all. Even my boys from football liked it. You might have to redesign their uniforms, too."

"Wow, thanks Ian. That means a lot," I said, beaming with pride.

At one point I could have sworn I overheard the girls behind me saying something about me. It was hard to discern exactly what they were saying, because the restaurant was so loud and my teammates were talking to me. And I admit, I shouldn't have been eavesdropping. (But let's not forget my previously stated rule on this topic: see entry from September 14.) The thing is, when it comes to anything Titan related, I'm a little weak. One girl behind me said something about "Madison," and then "really great," and another said, "I know!" And then, just when I was about to have heart palpitations, I actually heard the other one say, "Katie's gonna freak!" I practically fell out of my seat! I wanted to crawl under the table and sidle up to them and be like, "Hey, guys! Whatcha talking 'bout? What's Katie gonna freak about? Huh? Huh?"

And then, just when there was a nice little lull in the

GIVE ME A 165!

conversation at our own table that would have made it a teeny bit easier for me to hear what the girls behind me were saying, a deep voice said, "Sup, chicas?" I turned and saw my eavesdropping opportunity was over. A crowd of jocks had rushed into the restaurant, and three of them were circling the table behind us, eyeing the two Titan BFFs like, um, steak.

"Mads? Where did your head just go?" asked Lanie.

I noticed that Jacqui, Evan, and Lanie were all looking at me.

"Oh, sorry," I said. "You know me. Zoning out as usual!" I said with an apologetic shrug. I didn't want to admit to my friends that my ego had gotten the better of me and I'd been dying to hear what these girls were saying about me. Especially since it related back to Katie Parker . . .

Jacqui turned to Lanie, her chin in her palm. "She does that a lot, doesn't she?"

"Oh, yeah. Sometimes I worry that she might never come back," Lanie said, smiling back at Jacqui.

"Uh, guys? I'm right here. I can hear you."

"Oh, you mean right <u>now</u> you can hear us? Well, it's about time!" said Evan.

The coolest part about the dinner is that now my three friends are actually kind of getting along. Coolio.

GIVE ME A 166!

But Mom and I aren't doing so well in the getting-along department. After dinner, she was floating on a cloud and singing the chants we'd done that afternoon while she checked her e-mail. And she was still wearing that RIDONCULOUS track suit. I don't know why, but it annoyed me so much, I wanted to scream.

"Hey, Mom?" I asked, sitting down on one of our rickety wooden kitchen chairs. "Now that we're home, do you think you can lose the tracksuit?"

"You don't like it? It's supposed to be the coach version of your uniform designs. Guess I'll leave the fashion stuff up to you from now on." She smiled.

"I don't know," I said, frustration mounting inside me. "The tracksuit is fine, I guess. It's just that . . . do you have to be, like, so out there?" I asked.

"Out there? I'm just showing my support for the team," she said. "Oh, by the way, I was thinking. Next time, when you're doing the 'victory' chant, I think we should switch things up a little—"

"Mom, do you think, like, maybe for two seconds we could not talk about cheer? Like a normal kid and her normal mom?"

"But I thought you'd be excited about tonight, hon. I'd assumed you'd want to replay it all together."

"I _am_ excited," I said. "I'm just really tired. And kind of cheered out for the day, you know?"

"All right," she said, looking at me. "Mads, why don't you go upstairs and retire. It's been a long day."

I can tell she's hurt, but I don't have the energy to turn this one around. It definitely has been a really LONG day. So I trudged up the stairs to my room and collapsed on my bed, still in my uniform. I wish I wasn't so annoyed at Mom all the time, but it just seems like lately, at every opportunity, she does something that really gets to me. I def don't like this feeling.

GIVE ME A
168!

I guess I expected people to come up and congratulate us on how great we were last night, but the truth is, it's not like we were better than the Titans even on their worst day. I should just be happy that no one made fun of us or drew pictures of bears in cheerleading outfits on the chalkboards like they've done in years past. But a part of me would like a little bit of appreciation, thankuverymuch. We've come a long way with all the hard work that Jacqui and I and, ok, Mom have put into the team. Jared now restrains himself from wearing a top hat to practice (most of the time), Tabitha Sue has been meeting with Mom one-on-one to work on her chanting voice to make sure it doesn't squeak so much, and even the T-twins have started to appreciate the new kinds of muscles they've been building by supporting me and Jacqui as

GIVE ME A 169!

flyers. "This is better than weightlifting," Matt even said the other day.

Our humble victory (if you can even call it that) was kind of overshadowed by the Titan cheerleaders' big win at the cheerleading competition the night before and, of course, the actual soccer match. The soccer boys were crowded around the cheerleaders' table at lunch, flirting and throwing fries at them. I could hear giggles and cries of "Eww!" from across the lunch room and convinced myself I wasn't jealous at all that Bevan was part of that circle. Nope, not even one iota. (Yeahhhh, riiiight.) I am happy to note that even though Bevan was at the cheerleading table, he looked pretty bored. (But, just to be clear, it's not like I'm stalking him or anything like that.)

At the end of lunch, Clementine sauntered up to our table. She took this big ol' dramatic pause to make sure that we were all paying attention to her, and cleared her throat loudly. Evan, Lanie, and I looked up in surprise—like you do when a bride walks down the aisle or royalty enters the room. (Not that we have that in this country, but you get the drift.) Evan actually had a fry dangling out of his mouth. A Titan has never come up to our lunch table. Not in the entire history of, like, lunch. I guess I should start getting

GIVE ME A 170!

used to Titans surprising me all over the place now. It's starting to become, like, a regular thing.

"Madison," she said, looking at me with a mild level of disgust, "the Titans have something they'd like to discuss with you." She raised her eyebrow at the word "discuss." Taking in another deep breath, she continued. "Come by our side of the gym before practice." Before even waiting for a response, she did a kind of runway turn, fluffed her hair, and sauntered back to her table. A number of kids at nearby lunch tables looked on as if they were witnessing the eighth wonder of the world.

"Do you think she practices that eyebrow lift at home, kind of like an exercise routine?" said Lanie, spinning a carrot stick into a tub of hummus. "And lift and down and lift and down," said Lanie, lifting her eyebrow in time with her words.

Evan and I just laughed.

"It's so weird," I said. "Suddenly I'm, like, the Grizzly spokesperson. This is the second time a Titan has come up to me to ask me for a favor."

"Well," said Lanie, "if you need any, I can give you a couple of bullet points for your discussion with the Titans. For example, Clementine's choice of male company. Have you noticed all her ex-boyfriends are in remedial math and have names like chet or Brock?"

GIVE ME A
171!!

"No, Lanie. Actually, I hadn't." I laughed. "But I don't think the Titans will be asking me for advice on Clementine's taste in boyfriends."

All of a sudden the conversation I'd overheard at the Titan BFF booth at Steak & Fries came back to me. Those girls said something about "Madison" being "really great" and how "Katie's gonna freak." Just then it hit me.

My heart started beating fast. "Oh. My. God. Ohmigod, ohmigod, ohmigod!!! What if they want to talk to me about becoming a Titan?"

Lanie and Evan looked at each other and then at me, wide-eyed.

"There were these girls sitting behind us last night at Steak & Fries who are, like, Titan besties. I'm almost poz that I heard them talking about me. They probably saw the game last night and told the Titans what they saw in me . . . and maybe Katie, Hilary, and Clementine are finally giving me another chance!!!"

I felt like I was going to explode with happiness.

"Careful, daydreamer," said Evan, pointing a fry at me. "Don't get ahead of yourself. You never—"

"Wow. I, Madison Hays, might at the end of this very day become a Port Angeles Titan cheerleader!"

I can totally see it this time, and for once it doesn't seem that far-fetched. It will be hard at

GIVE ME A 172!

first, sure. We'll have a rough first few weeks as Katie, Clementine, and Hilary teach me the famously brutal Titan warm-up. I'll stay as late as possible to catch up on whatever they've been learning, but I know I can do it. Through our late-night practices, I'll learn that Clementine isn't really as mean and nasty as people think she is. She'll probably confide in me that she'd just had a really bad experience at cheer camp when she was a kid, and ever since then she's had to build up this big wall. I'll pat her on the back and tell her I understand completely but that she can totally be herself around me because I know the pressure that she's under and how sometimes it gets to be too much. Boy do I know.

I can't concentrate on anything the rest of the day. I couldn't wait to talk to the Titans. Everything I see starts looking like a cheerleader. In math class I was watching Mr. Hobart at the chalkboard when he started to morph

into a cheerleader with our white, red, and blue uniform. Next thing I knew, the blackboard became a game scoreboard and the scalene triangle Mr. Hobart was drawing became a megaphone. When he called on me to answer a question about perpendicular diagonals, I nearly answered in a chant. (But I have to say, I was pretty proud of myself for knowing the answer, since I could barely even concentrate on class. I had finally resolved to catch up on all my studying this past weekend. Give me a G-O, M-E!)

NIGHTTIME, MY BED

After school, I changed into my practice clothes and brought my pom-poms with me, just in case the Titans wanted me to do any on-the-spot demonstrations of my cheers.

But right as I was entering the locker-room area, Bevan and I nearly collided (again!) on his way to the weight room. He was wearing a fitted T-shirt that showed off those shoulders. I've been sketching pictures of him in my journal since our first collision. I'm doing a riff on Monet's <u>Haystacks</u>, but with Bevan's shoulders as the subject, at different times of day and in different light.

"Hey," he said, hanging onto

A. Bevan's shoulders when approaching from the lunch room

GIVE ME A 174!

the side of the concrete gym wall
and swinging his body lazily through
the entryway. "You guys were good
yesterday."

B. Bevan's shoulders
in line at the water
fountain

I was so stunned that he was
actually talking to moi that my "Oh,
thanks!" (which was supposed to sound
all smooth and confident) fell somewhere between a
squeak and a burp. The last time he'd addressed me
was during our first meeting on the sports field. (I
refuse to count the time he sort of looked at me
when I was in the car with Mom and she pointed at him,
since I'm still pretending that never happened.) I'd been
waiting for this moment for, like, ever, and now it was
taking me completely by surprise.

A slow smile crept onto his face,
revealing his adorable dimples, as he
waited for me to say something.

"Anyway," he said, looking at me
for a few seconds more. I just
stared right back at him like a mute

C. Bevan's shoulders
from behind

because I couldn't think of a witty follow-up to
continue this conversation. Actually I couldn't think of
ANY follow-up, witty or not.

"Later, Madison," he said, loping off in that way

GIVE ME A
175!

cool guys always do. Like they always have somewhere important to be but there's no rush to actually get there. On the other side of the spectrum, there's me. I'm usually just kind of making a lot of jerky, spazzy movements while standing in one place.

What is wrong with me? Do I need an official invitation to talk??

> Dear Madison,
>
> Here is that cute boy you've been pining for all these weeks. He'd like to talk to you. In fact, he's paying you a compliment right now. If you'd like, you may take this opportunity to say something back. Preferably something that has to do with the subject at hand. Oh no? You'd rather just stand there like an idiot? Fine, be my guest.
>
> Signed,
> Your Heart ♡
>
> P.S., You will be lonely forever and live with ten cats. And your mom.

I sighed and tried to put my game face on. I'd worry about Bevan later. My life was about to change. I could hear the Titans in the gym, chatting away. I went over to Clementine, since she's the one who approached me at lunch.

GIVE ME A 176!

"Hey. So, you wanted to talk to me?" I asked, supernervous. I pulled on a pom-pom string too hard, picking it free.

"Ohmigod, yeah," said Clementine, who grabbed me by the elbow and practically dragged me over to where Katie stood. Then I saw Clementine's gaze drop to my pom-poms.

"Oh, sweetie, you won't be needing those," she said, pointing to them.

"Oh, ok!" I said, putting them on the floor. "So, you just want me to do a cheer and dance routine, then?" I looked around for an iPod deck but didn't find one. Oh, well, I could wing it. I motioned to the pom-poms. "I brought these just in case you wanted me to incorporate them into my cheer. But I can work without them, no prob." I assumed a cheer position, with my legs apart and my hands straight at my sides.

"Um," said Clementine, "we don't need you to cheer for us. We didn't ask you here to recruit you. Like, seriously?" she said, looking at Hilary and then at Katie. "Ohmigod, no." She burst out laughing.

My heart dropped to my knees, and I could feel my face go beet red. I was sooooo embarrassed, I wanted to run right out of the gym and hide inside my locker for the rest of the year.

GIVE ME A
177!

"We actually wanted to talk to you about those amazing uniforms you designed for your squad," said Katie, shoving her friend in the ribs. "We think they're awesome. My friend took some pics on her iPhone at the game and sent them to us, and well, we would die to have uniforms like those for the Titans, too. I know it might be a little weird, but . . . we were thinking, maybe you could design something for us?"

"Oh, uh. I guess, maybe . . . really? My uniform designs?" I stammered.

"We'll tell everyone you're the designer, of course. It would mean a lot to our team," said Katie.

Clementine raised her eyebrow, sort of like to say, "You don't really have a choice."

I think I must have gone into some kind of cheer-induced shock, because I can hardly remember what happened next. I had my hopes set so high on being recruited by the Titans that being asked to be their clothing designer was the farthest thing from my mind. It was like being at the top of a pyramid and then falling flat on my face. And this time, there was no gorgeous Bevan Ramsey looking over me.

I do remember the Titans being really excited, jumping up and down, exclaiming that their new uniforms were going to be "the hottest." I also remember Hilary

GIVE ME A 178!

saying she couldn't wait to wear them to the next game, so I guess I must have said that I'd do it.

I walked back to the Grizzly area of the gym and was grateful that no one from my team had been there to witness what had just gone down.

Then it all started to make sense. The uniforms. That's what the girls had been talking about at Steak & Fries. That's what Katie was going to "freak" about. Not me or my cheer skillz. What had I been thinking?

All through practice, I was in a total daze. I kept thinking about how stupid I must have looked when I walked up to them with my pom-poms and this cheery expression on my face. And the awful way Clementine had laughed . . .

Jacqui wanted to teach the team power jumps, but I was like, "Can't we just do a regular ol' practice? I'm not feeling anything fancy." And for the first time ever, I didn't feel like staying after practice to work with Jacqui.

Jacqui walked back with me to the locker room, peering at me as if an alien had invaded my body. And I don't blame her—I'm not one to ever back down from taking things to the next level.

"What was up with you at practice today?" Jacqui asked me as she grabbed a fresh towel from her locker.

GIVE ME A
179!

I thought about maybe not telling her what happened with Clementine and Katie just before. But then I figured if there's any cheerleader who will understand what I've just been through, it's Jacqui. When I was done telling her what happened, Jacqui was like, "Whoa. That sucks."

I sat on the bench in the locker room, just shaking my head. "Right now I just feel like a giant idiot." I could feel the tears bubbling up in my eyes.

"You? An idiot? Please. It's those girls. . . ." I could see Jacqui start to get superangry, like she wanted to punch a wall.

"I wanted to be a Titan so badly," I said despondently.

"Madison," Jacqui said, "Clementine knew what she was doing when she came up to you at lunch. She's a calculating person, and she chose her words very carefully. She wanted to see you fall." Jacqui had a look on her face that told me this wasn't the first time Clementine had set someone like me up to look stupid.

"Well, either way," I said, "I guess this means the closest I'll ever get to being a Titan is being their clothing designer. My life's dream," I said, twirling my finger in the air with mock excitement and wiping the tears from my face.

GIVE ME A 180!

When I got home, Mom was all over me about my attitude at practice too.

"I just don't feel like talking about it, ok?"

"Madison, you're the co-captain of this team. You have to have a good attitude at practices," she said, placing some reheated Chinese food on the table.

"Mom, didn't we just talk last night about <u>not</u> talking about cheer when we're at home?"

Mom sat down across from me. T.G. she wasn't wearing last night's tracksuit or I would have lost it. SERIOUSLY lost it.

"It's just that you've been acting a little strange lately, Mads. You've been angrier than usual. And today at practice, you completely weren't yourself."

I don't know what came over me, but I blurted out, "Maybe I'd be able to be more myself if you weren't <u>trailing</u> my every move. Do you ever think about that, Mom? Do you know any other kids who spend morning, noon, and night with their moms? You're here in the morning when I have breakfast, you're my coach at cheerleading practice, and then, when I'm <u>home</u>, you either follow me around with ideas about cheerleading or you nag me about my stupid <u>ATTITUDE</u>! Sometimes I just need a break!"

Mom just sat there, listening to my rant patiently.

GIVE ME A 18!!

"Are you finished?" she asked.

"Yes," I mumbled into my sautéed string beans and shrimp. Just getting that off my chest made me suddenly feel a lot better. Like this pressure behind my neck had been taken away.

"Well, I'm glad to know how you feel, Madison. I just wish you'd told me somewhat . . . differently. It seems like you've been carrying this around for a while."

"Yeah, I guess I have. It's been building up."

Mom gave me a half smile with her naturally cherry-stained lips, the kind that only need a spot of gloss to look like she's wearing the perfect lipstick stain. "You've given me a lot to think about."

I don't really know what she means by that, but I hope it means she's gonna stop bugging me about cheer stuff when we're at home. The thing is, I know that actually isn't why I got mad at her tonight. Tonight I'm mad at myself. I'd gotten THIS close to being a Titan, or at least in my head I had, and then Clementine basically sat on my dream and squashed it with her oh-so-perfect butt. But what I want most of all is to be able to tell Mom all about what happened today. She'd totally understand. More than Lanie, more than Jacqui. No one on Earth shares my dreams of me becoming a Titan more than Mom. And, of course, the one person

GIVE ME A
182!

who I want to talk to about it the most is the one person I just screamed my head off at.

Nice going, Mads.

I know it's going to take forever to fall asleep tonight. I hate nights like this.

GIVE ME A
183!

Spirit Level:

Who Do We Appreciate? ←

Friends!

Yay for friends! Lanie and E are the best. When they started receiving one-word texts from me late Friday night, they sensed I needed a friendervention. It didn't take much guessing for them to figure out that my little rendezvous with the Titans didn't exactly turn out as I'd hoped.

"We R taking U to ur mothership," Lanie texted me Saturday morning.

"Gym?" I texted back warily, because that is soooooo not the way to cheer a girlfriend up. (No pun intended!)

"No, weirdo. The mall. 1pm, Hot Trax, b thr."

Evan had taken off from work at the comic book store, and Lanie was going to skip out on a reading by one of her favorite spoken-word performers at the local library. (Yes, she's for real.) I couldn't believe they did that just for poor, loser-y, me.

GIVE ME A
184!

"I don't know what I'd do without you guys, you know that?" I said when I met up with them in front of Hot Trax. Hot Trax is the number one spot to see and be seen at the mall. It's basically one of those T-shirt stores where they sell gag gifts and apparel related to pop culture or whatever It Band is "it" at the time. I can't remember the last time I bought anything there. I think we all just go there to see who's around.

"Yes," said Lanie, nodding her head vigorously. "Yes, we know."

We were just browsing around when . . . behold!! Guess who I saw checking out the retro T-shirts? My heart. My love. My one and only. Bevan Ramsey. Lanie registered the heat rushing to my face when I noticed him. "Do you need me to get you an ice bucket or something?" she said loud enough for the whole store to hear.

"Shh!" I whispered, running to hide behind the nearest rack. First of all, the last thing I'd said to him hardly qualified as English. Second of all, I was sure my humiliation with the Titans had gotten around to all their friends by now. No way did I feel like making a fool of myself in front of him today.

"Ohmigod. What do I do?" I said, frantic.

"Um, you could try talking this time," she answered.

GIVE ME A
185!

"Let him know you're actually not a mute. That should earn you some points back."

Before I could speak, she pushed the rack aside and looked at me like I was a badly behaved child screaming at the top of my lungs in a department store.

"Madison Jane Hays, get out from behind that death metal T-shirt this instant!"

Evan came sauntering by holding a Boys II Men lunch box. "How old school is this?" Then he poked his head into my hiding spot. "Hey, Madison, what are you doing?"

"Oh, nothing," I said, pretending to admire a T-shirt with a bloody skull on it. "I was just, uh, getting a closer look at the silk-screening. Thinking of taking it up as a hobby. Think of all the money we'd save on T-shirts, huh, guys?"

"Mm hmm," said Lanie, unconvinced.

I sighed and shuffled out of my hiding space only to find that Bevan was right around the corner by the sneakers. But before I could bolt out of there, he'd already locked eyes on me.

Those root-beer-colored eyes. Sigh. (BTW, just to clarify, root-beer-colored things, like eyes, are good. Not to be confused with root-beer-**FLAVORED** things, like gummy worms, which are bad. Very, very bad.)

"Hey Madison, what's up?"

Lanie quietly moved to another part of the store, leaving the two of us alone. (Evan was lurking nearby—I could see him out of the corner of my eye—but I tried not to focus on that.) "Just, you know." I shrugged. "Shopping."

"Cool." He nodded. "Me too. Me and my boys." He pointed over to his friends from soccer who were fooling around with some figurines. "You here with friends?"

"Yeah, but they, uh, seem to have disappeared or are busy being weird. Or both." I had a momentary freak-out of "so, what should I say right now?" but then I reasoned that since Bevan plays soccer, that's a safe subject. "So, you guys are having a good season, huh?" I asked.

"Yeah, it's cool. I'm proud of the team," he said modestly.

GIVE ME A 187!

Awkward silence.

"I see you and Jacqui have been hanging a lot after practice," he said.

I couldn't stop thinking, "He's noticed me! OMG, he's noticed me!!!

"Yeah, she's an awesome cheerleader," I said. "I'm really happy that she joined our team. She's taught us a ton."

"Yeah, she's pretty cool. It's crazy what happened with her and the Titans," he said. "Tough break."

So sweet of him to care ☺.

"Yeah, it seemed pretty rough on her," I agreed. "But she's pretty happy, I think." I shrugged.

"Oh, I meant to ask you something the other day," he said. One of those amazing dimples of his began to show, and my heart started to beat really fast again.

Finally! This was the part where my life would turn around. Bevan was going to ask me to go to every dance until the end of the year. No, until the end of school! Or to marry him! Yes, Bevan, I, Madison Jane Hays, do take you, oh-perfect-looking-soccer-player, to . . .

"How's it feel?" he asked, staring at my face.

"What?" I asked, confused.

"Your nose. How's it feel—you know, since I practically ran you over? It looks like it healed

GIVE ME A 188!

perfectly." He was doing it again—staring inches away from my face.

I could smell his shampoo from that close. It smelled like lavender with a hint of mint. I had to hold my hands down at my sides to restrain them from not reaching out and ruffling his mop of hair.

Suddenly, I heard someone clear his throat loudly behind me. Bevan instinctively straightened up and put his hands in his jeans pockets.

"Dude, we're heading to Sneaker City. You comin'?" said the throat-clearing soccer friend.

"Yeah, man, be right there," he said with a quick nod of his head. "So, I'll see you around, Madison, I guess."

I picked up some stationery that was on a nearby table, just to have something in my hand. "Yeah, later," I said.

"Have fun, uh, shopping," he said, smiling toward the stationery I was holding. When I looked down, I saw I was holding Hannah Montana stationery.

SERIOUSLY???

That is just so my life.

I looked for Lanes and Evan, and they were sitting outside Hot Trax sipping sodas.

"Whoa, girl. I didn't realize you had it that bad for this guy," Lanie said. "You really pulled out the stops: the hair twirl, the doe eyes, the giggle."

GIVE ME A 189!

"I don't know what the big deal is," said Evan, kicking around a discarded bottle cap. "He's just a stupid jock. Don't you hate those kinds of guys?"

"Bevan's not a jock," I said, grabbing Evan's soda from his hand. I took a long sip. "He's really nice."

"He almost gave you a concussion," said Evan. "And yes, you may have a sip of my drink."

Evan is usually a big sharer, especially when it comes to me and his food. It's, like, our thing. So he was being totally weird.

"That near-concussion was not on purpose," said Lanie.

Evan glared at her.

"What? I'm just stating the facts."

"Listen, we don't really need to argue about this. Yes, I have a crush. What's the big deal?"

"Nothing," said Lanie cheerily. "We just like giving you a hard time," she said, getting up from the mall bench. "Right, Evan?"

"Yeah, whatever," said Evan.

What got into Evan today? It's, like, what? Does Bevan use his puppy as a soccer ball or something? Suddenly Evan hates Bevan (ha, a new cheer!) with all his guts?

At least the mall excursion helped get me out of my funk. Friends + mall food + hot crush = cure for the blues any day.

GIVE ME A 190!

I should have seen this one coming a mile away, since Mom has been acting really weird all weekend. The telltale signs were there: the discarded spoons of Nutella in the sink, for one. Mom likes to keep a jar of Nutella in the cabinet, and whenever she has a craving she just has a tablespoon of the stuff. But when she's feeling depressed, she'll take a spoonful, put it in the sink, and then two seconds later decide she needs another. And another. So by the end of the night our sink is, like, blanketed in spoons that have each only been used once. One time I asked her why she just doesn't commit to one large spoon and have, like, a mini bowl of the stuff. "Because that would be disgusting, Madison," she huffed.

So anyway, there were the spoons of Nutella in the sink. And, Mom didn't sing a single chant all weekend. It

GIVE ME A
191!

was kind of like if you're used to having the radio on all the time, turned to a certain station, on high volume, and then all of a sudden . . . radio silence. That's what being around Mom was like this past weekend. Not one cheer. Not one "G-G-G-Grizzlies! We'll tear it up and tear it down!" Nothing.

We hadn't really talked since our little whatever-it-was on Friday night. Mom knows to give me my space after I act like that. But usually the next day we're totally fine. Not this time . . .

"Hey, Madison," asked Ian after warm-up. "Is your mom a bit under the weather today?" Chuckle, chuckle.

"Excuse me?" I said.

But I totally knew that Mom's 'tude wasn't going to be easy to hide from the rest of the team. She was practically broadcasting, "Hello! I'm in a foul mood. Make me mad or else." She didn't crack any jokes at the beginning of practice, and she was wearing this permafrown.

At the end of practice Mom was like, "All right everyone, I have to tell you something, and it's not going to be easy."

Oh, boy. This isn't going to be good.

Everyone on the team got into this circle around Mom and had these really serious looks on their faces.

GIVE ME A
192!

It was like she was about to tell us that someone died, or something like that.

"The Grizzlies are in a tremendously great place right now. I'm so proud of all of you. But I've given this a lot of thought," she said, folding her hands in front of her. "And I think coaching the Grizzlies isn't the best thing for me right now."

Everyone gasped. Everyone, that is, except for me, because I had a feeling once she said she had something to tell us that this would be it. I should have been relieved, but instead I felt incredibly guilty.

Tabitha Sue shot out from the group and threw herself against my mother. "Please, Coach Carolyn, don't leave us!" she pleaded.

My mom patted Tabitha Sue's back and smiled. "Oh, sweetie, I'm sorry, but this is for personal reasons. I have to do what's best for my family."

Gee, Mom, thanks for being so subtle. Couldn't you chalk it up to a mysterious disease or something? Sheesh.

I looked around the room and saw Jared was wiping tears away from his eyes. Katarina was muttering in Russian under her breath and looked like she was about to murder someone. Hopefully not yours truly. I couldn't believe Mom was going to give up the one thing that had

GIVE ME A
193!

made her happier than I'd seen her in years. I mean, even though a few days ago I'd strongly hinted that she do exactly that. But I didn't think she'd actually listen to me!

"Mom, please don't leave us," I said. "We need you."

Everyone nodded earnestly.

"I've made my decision, and that's that," Mom said, a bittersweet smile on her face. "I'm sorry," she said, choking up a little. "But I have to go." And before we knew it, she'd turned and left.

Apparently, Ms. Burger must have already known, because she came marching down the bleacher stands, looking quite unhappy. She hated to interrupt her LOLcat fanzine writing to have to interact with a group of misfit cheerleaders.

"Sorry, folks. You're back to dealing with me again," she apologized, her hands on her hips.

We all sighed wearily. With Mom as coach, at least we were taken a little more seriously at games. Now, with Ms. Burger again, we'd go back to being the school joke. Neither Jacqui nor I felt like practicing after practice today, so we went to change in the locker rooms with everyone else. The tension there was thick as a hot fudge sundae, and the vibe was just as cold. And guess who it was directed at. Poor little me! Like

GIVE ME A
194!

I'm the one who went and told my mom to quit!

Finally, Jacqui broke the silence. "Maybe you could talk to her?" she said, looking at me all serious.

I was digging something out of my locker, but when I turned around I found myself facing three sets of imploring, pound-puppy eyes (Jacqui's, Tabitha Sue's, and Katarina's, respectively). You would have thought these girls had lost their mothers—not MY mother.

"Ok, ok!" I said, defeated. "I'll talk to her. I'll do my best."

All right. So, wish me luck! Hopefully the walk home will be enough time for me to figure out what to say. . . .

GIVE ME A 195!

Tuesday, October 19

Bedtime, my room

Spirit Level:

Hip Hip Hooray!

When I got home, just as I expected,
mom was wearing her bad mood outfit,
which consists of her faded blue robe with
the moons and stars (and a ton of bleach
stains), her hair pulled back in a high ponytail
and an elastic headband, oversize sweats,
and Isotoners. This outfit is reserved for
special occasions only (i.e., fights with my
dad, breakups with guys, days when we have
money problems, etc.).

"Whoa," I said, when I walked into the
living room. "It's that bad, huh?"

"Mads, I'm sorry, but it's been a long day."

"Yeah, I know." I sat down next to her on
the couch and grabbed a little blanket.

Mom looked surprised that I was sitting

GIVE ME A
196!

so close to her, and I noticed her face soften a little. I guess it's been a while since we've hung out.

"Did I make it hard for you today?" she asked, scanning my face.

"Well, uh . . . a little," I said, picking up a Girl Scout cookie from the coffee table. "A bunch of people think I'm the reason you resigned."

Mom flipped through a bunch of TV channels, but I knew she wasn't watching (especially since she flipped right past a cheerleading competition without stopping).

"Oh, honey," said Mom. "I'm an adult. I value your input and suggestions, but no one makes me do anything. I saw that my being so involved in cheerleading was hurting you. You even kept coming to me, asking me not to do certain things. I think I pushed it a little too far because I was having so much fun. But I have to do what's good for you. I think, ultimately, this will be good for both of us." She smiled, patting my thigh.

I've been thinking about what, exactly, has been bothering me about Mom being my coach. Am I frustrated that I'm not as good a cheerleader as she used to be? Is it that I don't want my mom to be so involved in my school life? I realized, after she announced her resignation, that it isn't just one or the other. But what I know for sure is that I actually don't

GIVE ME A 1971!

want her to quit. What do I want are some boundaries.

"Mom, it's not that I don't want you as our coach," I told her. "You're the best coach the Grizzlies have ever had. Or could ever dream of having."

Mom smiled into her lap. "That really means a lot, Madison."

"I've been acting a little bit like a pain in the butt lately, Mom. I'm sorry."

"No, Madison, I think this coach thing was probably a bad idea for us. You were right to act out."

"No, Mom, I wasn't. I think you should come back to the team."

"Oh, Maddy," she said, shaking her head, "I love you so much. Thank you for saying that, but it just wouldn't be a good idea. . . ."

It took a while, but I pretty much begged Mom to reconsider being coach, and she said she'd think about it. (But the way she said it, I knew she was going to say yes.) We established some ground rules, so that in the future I won't get mad at her out of the blue. Like, when we are at home, we definitely won't talk about cheerleading 24/7.

"Say, when I'm trying to watch <u>So You Think You Can Dance</u>," I told her. "That's an example of a time when maybe you shouldn't bring up our routine for the

GIVE ME A 198!

chem league. I need a break sometimes."

"Ok, got it," Mom said, nodding in understanding.

I also asked her if this office-at-school thing was completely off the table. "Like I said, it's awkward for me to see you in the halls, you know?"

Mom looked at me like I was making some kind of joke. "But why? Other kids have parents on the faculty. What's so strange about it?"

"Well, it's not like you're an ordinary faculty member, Mom," I said, pointing to her perfect hair, face, and body. "You're a cheerleading coach. You're not, like, a teacher."

Mom looked offended. "I teach. I just teach . . . cheerleading!"

I gave her a look to let her know that I didn't exactly think of that the same way as teaching, say, math or English. She got the hint. "Can't we just keep it like, you coach the team during coaching hours and that's it? I'm feeling just . . . like it's too much sometimes."

Mom looked at me for a few seconds and then spoke. "Of course, Madington. You know, I didn't know how badly I wanted to do something related to cheerleading again—besides coaching you—until this opportunity came up. I guess I got really excited when

GIVE ME A 199!

you asked me to be the Grizzlies' coach."

"I know," I said. "And I feel a little guilty asking you to _not_ be as excited."

"Hon, that's not what you're asking me. You're asking me to just not be as in-your-face. I can do that," she said, patting my leg.

"Oh, and one more thing?" I said.

"Yes?"

"I know how to research online. And how to run fund-raisers. Basically, anything not related to actually cheering, I can probably handle on my own. I love that you try to help—but I need to be able to do this stuff on my own. Ok?"

Mom smiled. "I'll take a big step back," she assured me. "From now on, I'll leave you to your own devices."

"Ok, deal," I said, putting my hand out to shake on it. But instead, Mom grabbed it and pulled me into a hug. Aw ☺.

So, then I **FINALLY** told Mom about the whole thing that happened with Clementine and the Titans and how they wanted me to design their uniforms. I realized that's another thing that's been bothering me. I'm so used to telling Mom, like, everything related to cheerleading, and I've been holding this back.

"So weird, right?" I asked after I was done telling

GIVE ME A 200!

the story. "What do you think? It's good that they at least noticed my design skills, even though, I mean . . . it would have been nicer if they recognized my other skills."

"I think it's really great that they liked your designs," she said. But I could just tell in her face that she also wished the same thing I had: that the Titans wanted me to cheer, not to design.

Then, as if reading my mind, she says to me, "I know it's not the same as being a Titan, but maybe it's a step in that direction. You know?"

I hope she's right.

"Besides," she continued, "you've put so much hard work and effort into making the Grizzlies a real cheerleading squad. Is that really something you're willing to give up on so quickly? If the Titans had asked you to join, how would you have felt about leaving the other Grizzlies in the dust?"

"I don't know," I told her. "I guess I never really thought about it."

"Well, you're a leader, honey. This is what leaders think about," Mom answered.

"I guess you're right, Mom. It would have been really lame of me to just bail on everyone. But the Titans are my dream! You know that. If my chance to join them

GIVE ME A 201!

ever actually comes, am I supposed to just pass it by to stick with the Grizzlies forever?"

"Only you can answer that," she said. "It's a good thing you have some time to think it over."

She was right, AGAIN. And from the looks of it? I'd have A LOT of time to think it over. . . .

So, apparently Mom drives a really hard bargain these days. I had to watch Splash and Groundhog Day in order to get her to officially say yes to being coach again. Not that I don't like mermaid movies, or even groundhogs. But I like my mermaid love stories animated, as in Ariel and Prince Eric.

Before I got into bed, I sent a mass text to the team letting them know that Mom—I mean, Coach Carolyn—is coming back. Almost everyone was awake, and they sent me a lot of "Woo-hoo!" and "!!!!" replies. Katarina said she wanted to invite my mother and me over her house for a traditional Russian Sunday brunch to celebrate. "We eat you for brunch" was the exact sentence, but I think I know what she meant (I hope). Phew. Now my teammates won't hate me forever for making their dream coach leave the team.

And then Jacqui wrote, "Awesome, Mads. Knew u wld pull thru. BTW, R U gonna design the Titan uniforms 4 sure???"

GIVE ME A
202!

"Yep. I might slip on the measurements on Clem's uni 4 funsies . . . JK," I wrote back.

The screen was blank for a while. And then . . .

"Want me 2 submit the design 4 u?" she wrote.

Score! One less thing to worry about. I'm clueless when it comes to that stuff, and Jacqui did such a good job with our uniforms. So, awesome!

"YES!!! Thaaaaaaank uuuuu!"

Tonight for the first time in a while, I have a feeling that finally, everything is in balance. Mom and I are all good. Jacqui is going to help me with the uniforms for the Titans. And the Titans, well, at least they know who I am. And best of all . . . Bevan said hi to me today ☺.

GIVE ME A
203!

After practice, home, sweet home

Spirit Level!

Give me a DIS-AS-TER!

Seriously. A girl can't rest for a day?! Ok, fine, it's
already been more than a week, but still! The uniforms I
designed for the Titans came in today, and boy were we
all in for a surprise! But not in a good way. Ohhhhh, no. I
was there when they opened them because it was right
before practice started, and guess what? The uniforms
didn't look like what I designed at all! The colors were
the right colors, but instead of saying "Titans" they
said "Tight Ends." It gets better (or worse, rather).
The tops of the uniforms have shoulder pads, like some
kind of cheerleader meets football player meets 1980s
secretary! I was wondering if this was some kind of
joke?! My design SO did not have shoulder pads. Hello,
Dynasty much? Hilary was actually stupid enough to go
and try one of the uniforms on just to "see what it
looked like," and when she came out, the rest of her

GIVE ME A
204!

team couldn't stop laughing.

"Shoulder pads are coming back, aren't they?" asked Hilary, looking at her teammates for approval.

"Ohmigod, no, not on us," said Clementine. "Where's that Madison girl? I am going to kill her."

I'd been standing by the sidelines during the uniform reveal, so when I heard this, I quickly ducked behind the bleachers. I was going to be cheerleader roadkill for sure. Clementine would find me here, strangle me with some pom-poms, and leave me to rot. I decided to just hold tight for a while and send an SOS text to Jacqui to find me when she came to practice.

Jacqui found me there shaking in my sneakers. She was red-faced with laughter and clutching her belly.

"Are you not freaking out? How hysterical is this? It's exactly what you wanted—only better! Their big game is in three days, and they're stuck wearing those!" She pointed to one of the Titan cheerleaders, who was holding up one of the uniforms and frowning.

"Hide me," I said, hiding behind Jacqui until we got

to where our team was assembled. "I just don't understand! Wait, what do you mean, it's what I wanted?" I asked, throwing my hands up in the air. "My designs were so cool. How did they get turned into something with shoulder pads? And Tight Ends . . . really?"

Me: DEAD.

Jacqui just stood there, smirking.

Then it dawned on me: Jacqui did it. She altered them. Either that or some random dude at the uniform company was having some major fun at the Titans' expense.

"Jacqui, you did this?"

"Maybe," she said, not looking me in the eye.

"Why? Why would you make me look bad like that?"

Jacqui looked completely surprised. "I didn't make you look bad. I'm making them look ridiculous. I did it for both of us. Besides, you were the one who made that comment about altering Clementine's uniform. I thought you'd get a kick out of this."

"That was a joke! I wrote 'JK'! 'JK' means just kidding!! And what do you mean, you did it for both of us?" I was so confused. All I knew was that the Titans had asked me to do them a favor based on the fact

GIVE ME A 206!

that they thought I was talented at designing. And now even that was ruined for me.

"I saw you that day, in the gym, when they asked you to design the uniforms. You thought they were going to invite you onto the team. And instead they crushed you. And Clementine laughed that wicked laugh. I just couldn't stand by and watch you get hurt by them the way they hurt me," she said, scuffing her sneakers against the floor. "And I thought you'd be happy. Or at least laugh about it," she said flippantly.

"I'm _not_ happy. I'm megaembarrassed. But I guess I can see where you were coming from, and on some level I appreciate you looking out for me, but not this way. They're going to blame _me_ for this! You have to tell them what happened," I pleaded. A part of me was touched that Jacqui tried to defend me against the Titans. But the other part of me was really mad that she did it at my expense. She made me look like a real jerk in the process.

"Oh. I thought they'd just think it was a mistake with the factory," Jacqui said as she chewed a fingernail.

"Um, to quote, Clementine said, 'I am going to kill her.' And by 'her,' she meant _me_."

Jacqui agreed to talk to the Titans about her little

GIVE ME A 207!

switcheroo. Man, I've been doing a lot of negotiating lately. It's exhausting!

We told the rest of the team to get started on some warm-up moves. "Hey, Jared, can you lead the team through some stretches?" I asked him. "Jacqui and I just have to go take care of something."

Jared looked overjoyed to be the center of attention. "At your service, ladies," he said, taking a deep bow. "All right, team, get ready for some hip thrusts. Let's warm up our core!"

We could hear Ian and Matt groaning in protest as we left our side of the gym to walk toward the Titans. Mom looked on curiously, but knew I'd explain it to her later.

The Titans were in a tizzy over their botched uniforms. For the first time in, oh, I don't know how long, they hadn't started practice on time. Even Coach Whipley was sitting on the bench as if she didn't know what to do with herself. Uh-oh. This was bad news bears.

Katie was on her cell phone—with the uniform company, I assumed.

"There is no way that this was the design we ordered," she was saying in a measured but commanding tone. "No, I did _not_ specifically ask for shoulder pads.

GIVE ME A 208!

sir, sir, can I speak to your manager, please?"

When Clementine saw me, she pointed an angry finger at me and shouted, "There she is! Let's ask her what she did to our uniforms!" This was just great. Was the rest of the team about to descend upon me wielding pom-poms and pitchforks?

I quickly cowered behind Jacqui and gave her

a nudge. "That's your cue to start fessing up!" I whispered to her.

"Ok, I can explain," Jacqui said after what felt like five minutes.

Jacqui told the team how angry she'd been about

GIVE ME A 209!

why and how they'd ousted her from the team. "It was really uncool of you to make assumptions based on what you saw in my bag, not to mention the fact that you snooped in my bag to begin with! I still don't even understand how all of you missed the part where it said prescription," she said, a little hotly.

"Actually, Jacqui," said Hilary, "it was just Clementine who saw your pill bottle. We just went along with what she told us."

Clementine shot Hilary a dirty look. Hilary just shrugged like, "Hey, it's the truth."

"And we shouldn't have just gone along without questioning it," said Katie.

"Yeah, I can't believe that you didn't just come up and ask me about it. Instead you started spreading rumors. And the next thing I know, you tell me I'm not needed anymore—in front of everyone. So, I offered to submit Madison's designs for your team, and I kind of added my own, um, finishing touches. I realize now that it was a really bad idea. It's just that . . . we used to be so close," said Jacqui, her arms crossed defensively across her chest.

Katie went up to Jacqui and put an arm on her shoulder. "I'm really sorry, Jacqs. We let things go overboard. We were so caught up in getting to

GIVE ME A 210!

Nationals, we let ourselves get convinced that you had a problem. Also, to be honest, I think we were all intimidated by you. You got so much better over the summer, the rumor made us feel a little better about ourselves," she said, looking pointedly at Clementine.

Clementine just turned her back on the scene.

"As Titan captain, I apologize on behalf of the rest of the team for our behavior. And I'd like to offer you a place back on the team. That is, if you'll take it," she said, looking at Jacqui imploringly.

I got a little nervous because I wasn't really sure what she'd say. For a second I was thinking, "Hey, that was a nice apology," and maybe she'd go back to them. I wouldn't blame her at all. It was my dream to be a Titan, too, and if they had actually asked me to join instead of asking me to design their uniforms, I totally would have jumped at the chance. But as long as I'm a Grizzly, I (selfishly, I admit) want Jacqui on my side.

Jacqui was smiling from ear to ear. "No, thanks."

Hurrah!!!

"The Grizzlies need me right now. I'm happy where I am. But I appreciate your asking."

Katie nodded, understanding.

I did little cartwheels in my head.

Meanwhile, Clementine's head was about to blow

GIVE ME A
211!

off. "This is all very heartwarming, but has everyone forgotten that we have a game on Friday night and no uniforms? Someone had the bright idea to donate our old ones to charity—ahem, Hilary—and now we have a whole team of cheerleaders without anything to wear. Unless, of course, you think shoulder pads are, um, 'totally in,'" she said in a mock valley girl voice.

"What about wearing our uniforms?" I blurted out without even thinking. It was like someone had taken over my body and just vomited out words. Weird. But suddenly, I had a whole Titan brigade looking at me. Ahhhh! "I mean, you guys like them so much. And I know they don't say 'Titans,' but we do represent the school. . . . It's better than nothing, right?"

Radio silence. I was speaking English, wasn't I?

"This is so not happening," said Clementine, turning away again. Interesting strategy, BTW. (Mental note: Perhaps I should try this at future dining experiences with Dad and Beth.)

"I don't know . . . it's not such a bad idea," said Katie matter-of-factly. "We can say we're doing it on purpose to support the Grizzlies. No one would question it. No one questions anything we do." She looked back at the rest of her teammates. "C'mon, guys. We're Titans. We can do whatever we want."

GIVE ME A 212!

Of course the rest of the team agreed with their fearless leader (even Clementine, although she wasn't thrilled). I did little backflips in my head, I was so happy my idea went over well. I didn't really want to think about what would have happened if the Titans didn't have uniforms for their next game. They probably would have still somehow blamed me, and then my shot at ever having a spot on the team would be zilch. Zero. Nada.

After practice, Katie, Jacqui, and I hung out in the gym to talk about the details of the Grizzly-Titan uniform switch. It actually was going to work out perfectly. We'd ended up having enough money to order two uniforms per person, so we even had enough boy uniforms for the Titan guys. (And luckily, by the time we had ordered uniforms for Ian and Matt, they'd lost some of their bulk from football season, so their uniforms would just about fit the Titan guys' lean frames.) It was nice to hang out with Katie and get to talk to her without Clementine and Hilary around. I mean, we didn't, like, get to bond over mud masks and scary movies, but I'd never had a whole conversation with her before. She definitely seemed to appreciate my helping out with her team's problem.

And it seemed like Jacqui was off the hook, too, T.G. From the way Katie and Jacqui were practically holding hands and walking down memory lane, it seemed

GIVE ME A 213!

like they were on their way to repairing their old friendship.

"Hey, remember when you were a flyer that one time," said Katie, "and you were about to do a cradle and then lost your balance and landed in Jenny's hair?"

"Ohmigod, and then we all fell on top of the back bases?" said Jacqui, her eyes wide at the memory. "That was hilarious!"

"And painful!" added Katie.

"How about that time when you fell out of the basket and everyone just walked away?" said Jacqui.

"That was just plain mean," said Katie, scowling. "You're lucky I'm a forgiving person." She smiled.

I half-expected them to start crying and hugging and planning trips to the mall. I was psyched to see that everything was cool between them—and that the Titans no longer have me on their Wanted Dead or Alive list. So, I'm back on track. I still have a shot, maybe, of one day making it to my favorite team. Even if it means having to stand being next to someone as horrible and conniving as Clementine Prescott.

GIVE ME A 214!

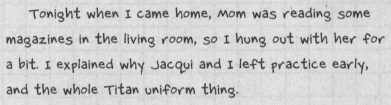

Tuesday, November 2

Evening, sofa city

Spirit Level:

Spreading Good Cheer

Tonight when I came home, Mom was reading some magazines in the living room, so I hung out with her for a bit. I explained why Jacqui and I left practice early, and the whole Titan uniform thing.

"Get out of here!" Mom said, slapping the arm of the couch. "That Jacqui." She laughed. "I could tell she had a wild streak in her."

I think I expected Mom to be a little disappointed or angry with Jacqui at what she did to the Titans. She takes cheer SO seriously, I would have thought she would say destroying a cheer uniform is next to, like, graffiti-ing the American flag. But she was laughing when I told her how ridiculous the uniforms looked and how the Titans reacted when they saw them. And she was glad that Jacqui came clean so that the Titans know I had nothing to do with messing up their uniforms.

GIVE ME A
215!

"It was the ultimate in team spirit, you know, sharing the Grizzly uniforms with the Titans," Mom said approvingly.

"Aw thanks, Mom." She thinks everything has to do with team spirit, **LOL**.

"Although I have to say, I wish I got to see what your design looked like. I mean, before it got . . . altered."

"I can show you," I said, reaching into my gym bag for my journal. "I have the sketches right here." It wasn't the same as seeing it rendered in fabric, but at least I was able to show her my idea.

"You're really something, Madington," said Mom,

blue stripe

red

back view

NEW Titans' uniform design

GIVE ME A 216!

admiring the sketches. "Ever since you could hold a pencil, you've been drawing clothes. You used to design outfits for your teddy bears. Do you know that?"

"No, I don't remember that," I said, flipping through my journal to show her another outfit I was working on.

"Oooh. Adorable!" she exclaimed. "You know, Mads, cheering isn't forever. Your future has so much in it, lots more than just cheerleading," she said, nodding toward the design on the page.

I looked at her face and saw it had gotten a little far-off looking.

"I might not have outgrown _my_ cheering phase, as you may have noticed." She laughed. "I'll admit it. But sometimes I think there are other things I should have pursued," she said with a faraway look in her eye.

Whoa! Who flipped the serious button?

"I get that, Mom. And I know there are other things out there for me, but right now, I'm really into cheer. It's my life." I shrugged. I don't really want to think about a future without cheering in it just yet.

Mom just looked at me kind of funny in that adult "you'll understand when you're older" kind of way. Whatever. Parents.

I jogged up to my bedroom and signed on to see who was on chat. Lanes was on, but Evan wasn't.

GIVE ME A 217!

"Whuddup, chica?" said Lanie.

I gave Lanes the lowdown on the afternoon, and when she was done cackling maniacally over the part when the Titans first saw their horrible uniforms, she offered up, "Mads, you totally should have made them wear those. We could have taken pics! We would have always had something to brighten our bad days!"

"Thanks, Lanie, that's really helpful. Remember, I'm trying to one day become a member of that team?"

"Oh, right," said Lanie. "But maybe you could just go back to your original idea of having an awesome uniform for everyone but Clementine?" said Lanie.

"Ha-ha-ha. Hey, what's Evan up to?"

Lanie shrugged. "Dunno. Prolly geeking out and writing some more SuperBoys. Hey, we were thinking of just selling some at the game. Not, like, for cheer fund-raising purposes but, um, fund-raising for just us. That ok with you?"

I'm more than happy for my buds to continue with the fund-raiser idea without fund-raising for cheer. It's Evan's creation, after all.

"Of course! Go nuts!"

I can share the wealth. It's been a big sharing day, after all.

Later on, Dad called. Apparently he wants to come

GIVE ME A 218!

watch the soccer game on Friday. So, he's coming with me and Mom (without Beth! Yippie!!), which hopefully won't end in World War III, but at least he's not insisting on watching me cheer at next week's chess club tournament. I have to draw the line somewhere.

GIVE ME A
219!

Friday, November 5

Afternoon, my room

Spirit Level!

Frozen Mid-Cheer

Hurrah!! Our team kicked butt and won—AGAIN!—
and the Titan cheerleaders stole the show with the
Grizzly Bears' uniforms! When they came running out
onto the field, everyone went crazy. At first people
didn't know what to make of it, and they were laughing
and whistling, "Yeah, Titans! Yeah, Grizzlies!" The
crowd thought it was hysterical. Katie even inserted a
little nod to the Bears into their routine by doing our
signature pencil jump with a little bear claw at the end
of it. (Yes, we have a signature move now!!)

Dad even seemed to enjoy the game—and didn't
say anything negative about cheerleading, which
was nice. He and Mom didn't fight AT ALL, which
was a miracle but also due to the fact that I
strategically placed Evan next to me, Lanie on my

GIVE ME A
220!

other side, and Dad and Mom on either end.

One downer: It was hard to fantasize about my future wedding to Bevan with Mom and Dad so close by. I'd be having a perfectly nice daydream in which Bevan was down on bended knee—socked knee and asking for my hand in eternal wedded bliss (or at least asking me to, like, a movie), and then Dad would ask a question about what kind of stunt the Titans had just done, or Mom would poke my leg and say, "Let's remember to try that one!" Ugh. Parents. Don't they have their own lives??

"I gotta admit, they wear those uniforms well," said Evan appreciatively.

"Ahem, I think I'll take that as a compliment to my work," I said. I don't know why it bothers me when he says stuff like that, but seeing Evan look at the cheerleaders like that, like, totally skeeves me out. I know it's weird, but seriously? **BLECH!**

"Did you keep the other uniforms for Halloween?" asked Lanie. "I'd wear one."

"Oh, yeah, like you'd wear a skirt ever," I told her.

"I said 'for Halloween'," Lanie replied, rolling her eyes.

Dad wanted to take me for ice cream after the game (an old tradition), but before we left I wanted to catch up with Jacqui in the gym lobby to say hi.

GIVE ME A
22!!

Dad and Mom walked off on their own to talk, which I tried not to worry too much about. You never know when a talk might end up with them flinging piles of dirt at each other.

Jacqui was by the water fountains.

"So, thank goodness that didn't end up in disaster, huh?" I said.

"Ohmigod, I know. When they first came onto the field, my heart was pounding. Like, I know they're the Titans and all that, but even this might go over everyone's heads."

"They pulled it off, like they always do," I said, shaking my head.

Just then, Jacqui got a funny look on her face, like someone was behind me. I turned and to my complete surprise saw Bevan standing there. In those adorable soccer cleats and shorts!!!

Maddy ♥'s soccer cleats

As Jacqui turned to walk away, she gave me this look like, "Watch out, girl," which I tried desperately to ignore.

I smiled at her and gave a little wave, suddenly feeling a million times more awkward than I had two seconds ago, before my true love was standing in front of me.

"Gr-gr-great game tonight," I stuttered. Why am I

GIVE ME A 222!

always so challenged around this guy?

"Thanks," he said. "So what was up with the Titans wearing your Grizzly getups?"

"Oh, that? It's a loooong story."

A couple of seconds passed. "Well, is it a long story you might want to tell me, like, next Friday night maybe?" A slight blush entered his cheeks.

"What's happening Friday night?" I asked. Like the total nerd that I am. Ding dong. Hello! Bevan was asking me on a date. Last time I checked, my big Friday night plans had been video chat three-way with Evan and Lanes. Which, don't get me wrong, is absolutely thrilling. Especially because that means we can hang out AND watch our favorite TV shows without having to compromise on a TV channel. But that's beside the point. . . .

"Sorry," said Bevan, pushing his hair out of his face with the back of his hand. "I meant, do you want to go somewhere Friday together? Like, a movie or something?"

"Oh." I blushed. "Yeah, sure. Definitely." I tried to play it cool and not smile from ear to ear. But I'm sure I looked something like this:

GIVE ME A 223!

"Cool," he said, showing those amazing dimples of his.

"Cool," I said.

"Cool," he said again.

We both laughed at the same time.

Yay! I'm not the only one around here who's a little challenged, I guess.

We said we'd figure out the deets sometime next week. I cannot **WAIT** to tell Lanes about this. She is going to freak out. Never in a million years did either of us think a superadorbs guy like Bevan would look at me twice, let alone ask me out on a date. But a lot of surprising things have been happening lately. Speaking of which . . .

I was about to leave the gym to go find Dad when I felt someone slap me on the butt. I whizzed around, expecting it to be, like, Ian or Matt being their usually jerky selves. Instead, it was Katie and Hilary.

"Hey, girlie!" said Katie, going in for a high-five.

Girlie?

"That was uh-mazing! Everyone loved your idea—could you hear the crowd?"

Katie's eyes were gleaming. Guess the girl was in a good mood. "I think we really took the crowd by surprise."

"Totally," said Hilary, adjusting the waistband on her

GIVE ME A 224!

skirt so even more of her perfectly toned midriff showed.

"But seriously, though, we still need new uniforms—which is why we need your help." Her voice got really grave and serious, as it always did when she talked about cheer stuff. You'd think we were talking about top-secret Pentagon things.

"Do you think you could submit your uniform design for us again? For real this time?" Katie winked.

"Of course," I agreed. Duh. First of all, I'd love to see another one of my designs come to life. Second of all, I kind of owe it to them after they'd just given the Grizzlies some good press.

"You're awesome," said Katie, squeezing my shoulder. "I told you we could rely on her," Katie said to Hilary, who just smiled back in that blank way of hers.

As I walked out of the gym into the cool fall air, I felt the best I'd felt in . . . well, ever. I'd helped Jacqui get back on track with the Titans. The Grizzlies are no longer the biggest school losers—well, not as big as we used to be. I am "in" with Katie Parker and her teammates. And the icing on the cake? Bevan Ramsey asked me out on a date! Me!

Wait a minute.

Oh no. Noooooooooooooooooooooooooooooooo! I stopped

GIVE ME A 225!

dead in my tracks. I remembered what Jacqui had told me a few weeks ago and that funny look she gave me when Bevan had walked up to me moments before. Katie Parker and Bevan Ramsey used to date, and **HE** dumped her. She still isn't over him. Which means if I go out with Bevan, I'll be Enemy #1 of the Titans.

And I'll never have a chance in a million years of ever wearing that prided Titans—or "Tight Ends"—uniform. Back to the point at hand . . .

My choice is plain and simple. I'll have to call off the date with Bevan if I ever want to fulfill my dream of one day being a Titan.

Sigh.

Oh, well. Who needs love, anyway, when you have a perfectly good (Ok, ratty old) pom-pom to kiss good night?

And cheer, lots and lots of . . .

CHEER!

GIVE ME A
226!

And now an excerpt from the next book in the series . . .

Monday, November 15:

After Grizzly practice, Port Angeles school locker room

Spirit Level:

Ready and (sort of) Ok!

The gym at Port Angeles School was even noisier than usual this afternoon when I met up with my cheer co-captain, Jacqueline Sawyer, to lug the boxes that had arrived at my house earlier this morning over to the rowdy group of cheerleaders in their designated corner. I couldn't wait to show the Titans the new uniforms I designed for their team—for **REALZ** this time. Well, I mean, I **DID** design them the last time—it's just that there was an itsy-bitsy mix-up when Jacqui submitted the designs to the uniform company. See, she kinda put her own spin on them so that when the Titans got their new uniforms, instead of saying "Titans" on the shirts, it read "Tight Ends." This was Jacqui's way of getting back at her old teammates for kicking her off the squad, but it also put me in a totally awkward position.

Here's what the uniforms looked like when I first handed the sketch over to Jacqui.

"new" "titans uniform"

ugh...

Jacqui's revenge!

And here's what they looked like after Jacqui had her revenge.

Ridiculous!! It looked like a football uniform married a cheerleader uniform and then had a baby uniform that went onto the discount rack at Filene's Basement. Total fashion faux pas.

Anyway, I made good on my promise to get the uniforms right this time, and thankfully, Jacqui stayed out of my way. Well, the truth is, she's back to (kinda) being friends again with Katie Parker, Titan head cheerleader and all-around Miss Perfect.

"Watch out, Grizzlies coming through!" cried Hilary Cho when she spotted us. Then she did a little roar, like a bear. Ha-ha. Get it? Grizzly Bears? Like I haven't heard that one before.

So, Hilary is the third girl in what my friends and I like to call the "Triumvirate" of the Titan cheerleaders: Katie Parker, Clementine Prescott, and Hilary Cho. Hilary pretty much just goes along with whatever Katie and Clementine think is cool. She's a total sheep. Baa, baa.

I hate it when the Titans get all snotty like that. I mean, the Grizzly Bears are cheerleaders too! Ok, so we're kind of at the bottom of the cheerleading food chain. We don't, you know, walk down the hall strutting our killer abs and supershort skirts. And until just recently, we were living in uniforms from, like, twenty years ago. Gross! We're not friends with the football jocks (so annoying) and we don't have prime real estate in the cafeteria (Ha! We're lucky if we have a table at all). See map of caf.

old grizzl
uniforr

GRIZZ

poop

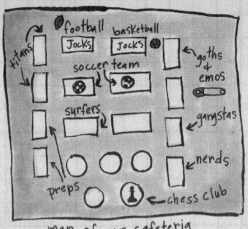

map of our cafeteria

Some might say we don't do or have those things because we are, like, so **ABOVE** that. Really? We don't because we can't. We're the B-team. The Grizzlies were formed because the school felt that no one should be turned away from wanting to participate in school-spirit-related activities. Anyone who doesn't make the cut for Titan tryouts automatically gets to be on the Grizzly squad. Hooray! So that's where we come in: We are the voice of the uncoordinated. We also come in handy when the Titans are so busy competing to get to Nationals that they can't cheer at our school's games. I mean, who else would cheer for debate team, chess club, or math league?

But still, there's no need for people like Hilary to rub it in our faces.

I'm far from uncoordinated, but I know I'm not quite

Nationals material. Still I'm a way better cheerleader than anyone on my team (except for Jacqui, obvs, but she WAS a Titan once, after all). My ultimate dream is to be a Titan. I just keep hoping that if I practice harder, learn the Titans' killer choreography, and hit every stunt, I'll be good enough to wear one of the uniforms I worked so hard designing for their squad.

It would be nice if I had more time to work on my clothing designs, though. Sometimes it feels sort of like an obsession. When I'm not sketching out new stunts for my team in this here journal, I'm pretty much designing clothes (and cheer outfits).

my never-leave-the-house without-it journal

"So, what's with the boxes?" asked Clementine, Triumvirate Member #2. "Make it quick. We're bugging out." (Ugh. Being on Clementine's bad side is never a good idea. Ever. She can cut you with just one nasty look, seriously. Once, she looked at a seventh grader funny and the girl broke out in hives!! For realz.)

I explained that I was about to present her and her team with new uniforms. Of course this got Clementine's attention. (Anything having to do with Clementine usually does.) She knelt down beside the box

I'd opened to grab one of the plastic-wrapped uniforms.

"Huh, this doesn't look like a disaster," she said, checking out the skirt appreciatively. This was a high compliment coming from Clementine. She smoothed the skirt against her spray-tanned legs. "Ooh, and it's short, too!"

I could just see her thinking about how great it will look on her when she prances down the halls of Port Angeles (as if she needs **MORE** guys looking in her direction).

"These are amazing!" squealed Katie, holding a uniform out in front of her. "OMG, Madison. Loves!"

She was literally smiling from ear to ear. Jacqui gave me a little wink.

"Awesome. Glad you guys like 'em," I said.

T.G. I'm **BEYOND** relieved. I mean, can you even imagine what would've happened if she'd, like, hated them? I couldn't mess up **AGAIN**!! Not with my future team captain (fingers crossed! ☺). Also, Katie and I have become more friendly just recently. I bet if I hadn't made these uniforms look perfect, she would've gone right back to ignoring me. No, thank you!

CUPCAKE DIARIES

Middle school can be hard...
some days you need a cupcake.

Meet Katie, Mia, Emma, and Alexis—together they're the Cupcake Club. Check out their stories wherever books are sold or at your local library!

CUPCAKE DIARIES

Katie and the cupcake cure

by coco simon

CUPCAKE DIARIES

Mia in the mix

by coco simon

Katie · Mia · Emma · Alexis

You're invited to a

CREEPOVER™

WE DARE YOU...
TO CHECK OUT THESE
TERRIFIC AND TERRIFYING TALES!

Truth or Dare...

You Can't Come in Here!

Published by Simon Spotlight • KIDS.SimonandSchuster.com

YAY!